Boracay Vows

CARPE DIEM CHRONICLES 1

MAIDA MALBY

Seize the day,
always!

EOT Publications

Carpe Diem

COPYRIGHT

Cover design by Render Compose
Edited by Linda Hill

First Edition: November 2017

To my loves, my heart, my home: this is for you.
Beloved Husband Brian and our son Stevie, Expert of
Things, I love you.

To foreign-born spouses of Americans who love to
read romance novels: This is for us.

ACKNOWLEDGMENTS

The number of people I have to thank for making my dream come true will fill the whole island of Boracay. I will not be able to name all of them here so I will just say thanks to everyone who supported me and encouraged me in the making of this book.

Massive thanks to the best book club in the world OSRBC, especially to my amazing editor Linda Hill, fabulous cover designer Lucy Rhodes, and wonderful Beta readers: Rizalee, Cecille, and Eva. Much gratitude to Rainne Mendoza (*Fobolous*) and R.G. Gallardo (Survivor series) for involving me in the creative process of their respective books.

Huge thanks also go to my cover team: my sister Myrtle and photographer-extraordinaire Celeste Odono. My gurus on this incredible world of Indie publishing: Linda Hill and Eva Moore deserve another mention. *Maraming salamat* to my *barkadas* UNYLACE, Chi Phi Pi, and Basic Burlesque for being the models for my characters. Thanks to Chiqui, Yulia, and N for helping me flesh out my plot.

Finally, and most importantly, the biggest of thanks goes to my husband, who is also my publisher, and my son for all the love and support.

SATURDAY

Chapter One

Barkada [bär-kä-də], n. – a group of friends.

I'm going to kill my friends! Krista fumed as she threw garment after garment onto the bed. She had planned to put her clothes into the wardrobe, but stopped when she saw the contents of her suitcase.

Skimpy two-piece bathing suits with matching sarongs were in one mesh laundry bag. Tank tops, tiny shorts, bikini panties, and thin summer dresses were folded neatly inside another. *I don't own these sexy things.*

Her gaze darted to the suitcase as another possibility occurred to her. "All the luggage on the carousel at the air strip looked alike. What if …"

She grabbed the tag to check if her bag was switched with someone else's and groaned to see the name written there was her own. Her head dropped in resignation.

"Yep, they're mine all right." The two other women on the flight with her couldn't have fit into these outfits. One was a matronly German lady, and the other was a tiny young Japanese woman. Although these clothes were not Krista's style at all, they were exactly her size.

This was what she got for giving her four know-it-all friends carte blanche regarding this trip. She didn't have time to attend to things, so she told her friends to go ahead and do what they wanted. Which they obviously did.

Throwing her hands in the air in surrender, Krista flopped down on the bed. "Scheming witches," she bit out without much heat. Her *barkada* really planned this to the last detail.

Maddie, Angela, Jenny, and Lisa took care of the flight, all the arrangements for her vacation, and even the packing of her suitcase. It was their gift for her thirtieth birthday—an all-inclusive eight-day, seven-night stay at a luxurious resort on the quieter side of Boracay, one of the most popular islands in the Philippine archipelago.

Her friends purposely ignored Krista's request not to send her somewhere expensive. Their choice was so posh, the place owned an air-taxi service to ferry its elite clientele from the city of Makati directly to and from the resort's air strip.

The original plan was to go home to her parents' province for the three-day All Saints' Day break, but the girls strong-armed her into making it a full week vacation somewhere else. Going to Quezon was too boring, in her friends' opinions. Since she had never been to Boracay, this was where they sent her. "Never mind that I don't like the beach, not to mention I hate getting tanned," she grumbled out loud.

With a shrug, she got up to put away the clothes, recognizing the futility of resisting something she couldn't change. She could hardly wear the outfit she had on now—a loose, white, short-sleeved polo shirt and black slacks—every single day, especially not in this heat. "At least I won't be naked, although I might as well be with these skimpy outfits."

Krista halted in front of the mirror and laughed derisively at her reflection.

"Yikes! Who goes to the beach wearing office clothes? Only you, Krista Lopez. Only you."

Her usual shapeless clothes, ponytailed hair, and wire-rimmed eyeglasses rendered the makeover her friends insisted she get nearly useless. Obviously, she did not belong in Boracay in her normal state. Krista removed her glasses with a self-pitying sigh.

Peering at her image more closely, she traced her eyebrows and winced in remembered pain at the plucking she had endured the previous day. Escorted by Jenny and Lisa, she'd had her bikini area waxed for the first time in her life, and her bush neatly trimmed.

Her friends pointed out that, had Angela and Maddie been there instead, they'd have insisted on a full Brazilian wax. *Good heavens!* The crazy duo smirked the whole time. They probably knew how skimpy all her new swimwear was.

Krista raised her right leg onto the stool in front of the mirror, rolled up her pants, and ran her hands lightly down the side. The silky-smooth feel of her skin made her smile. "Hmm, perhaps this pampering isn't so bad after all."

She straightened and removed her hair from its ponytail, fluffing it to fall softly around her face. It had been long and straight for so many years, she had forgotten it was naturally curly.

Vanity, thy name is Krista. Her lips twisted at the irony of that claim. Always being one to downplay her looks to discourage male interest, it became second nature to appear plain rather than enhance her natural beauty.

Krista wasn't the prettiest in the group, but she had the fairest and clearest skin of the five of them. It wasn't only a matter of genetics—she had a strict skin care regimen that included staying indoors as much as possible. Her uniform of long-sleeved blouses and suits helped to protect her skin from sun exposure.

Going to the beach was an out-of-the-ordinary event for her. Her friends knew this, yet here she was. On the beachiest beach in the country, no less.

Three loud raps on the door resonated across the cottage, making her jump. *Who could it be?* She didn't know anybody on the island.

Out of habit, she secured her hair back in its ponytail and donned her eyeglasses to meet the unexpected visitor.

"Sir!" Krista exclaimed. Mr. Blake Ryan, the hotshot chief executive officer of the manufacturing company she worked for, stood on the front patio of her beach cottage. Tall, tanned, and sexy, he embodied the type her friend Maddie usually dated and the kind her mother warned her to stay away from: overwhelmingly male and most importantly, a foreigner.

Almost everyone in the office—female or male, straight or gay, married or single—had a crush on him. *Oh yes, including me, although I shouldn't.*

When her employment recruiter arranged an interview at the company, she almost didn't go, knowing her new boss would be this young, good-looking American. But the position and its corresponding compensation package was too attractive to resist. She accepted the job, offered to her by Mr. Ryan himself, close to six months ago.

Since their first meeting, her awareness of him had threatened her self-imposed restrictions on romantic involvements. Her attraction went against everything her mother taught her. He made her nervous. He could break through her defenses, so she tried to keep her distance.

She had met other foreign men, but not one had made her heart beat faster when he drew near like this man. Right now, with only a couple of feet separating them, her heart was beating madly and all her senses were heightened. It was impossible to hide. Krista did not always lack self-confidence, but here in Boracay she was in unfamiliar territory.

"Hello, Ms. Lopez. I saw you pass by my cottage." With a smile on his face, he pointed in the general direction of the neighboring structure. "I wasn't sure it was really you, so I came to check."

Mr. Ryan wore a simple white t-shirt and khaki shorts, showing off his ripped chest and tanned, muscular legs. *He's the foreigner, but he looks so at ease, so at home.* This place suited him. *Me, not so much.*

Krista knitted her brows as his statement sunk into her befuddled brain. Already feeling insecure, she seethed at his question about her identity. Her stare went from one of appreciation of his fit body to one of resentment over the perceived insult. *It's fine for me to think I don't fit in here, but it's not okay when somebody else says it.*

"What do you mean you weren't sure it was really me? Don't you think I belong in a place like this?" Her voice had risen in volume to nearly a screech.

Who the hell does he think he is? He was the main reason she ended up here. Mr. High-and-Mighty CEO was going on leave and needed her input on some plans for the coming year by Thursday night the previous week, meaning she'd had to work overtime before her vacation.

His smile turned into a puzzled frown. "What? No!" He shook his head and held out his hands as if to ward off an attack.

Her hands were fisted by her sides, her weight shifted forward. A sane voice inside her head scolded her for acting crazy, but she ignored it. *Yeah, he's the boss, but we're not in the office now. He could hardly fire me for getting mad at him for judging me, could he?*

"I apologize, Ms. Lopez. I didn't mean it the way you took it. I thought it was you from the way you're dressed, but the shorter hair made me doubt it. Your fairness also made me think you don't go to the beach often." The tone of his voice was calm and reasonable; all his earlier warmth was gone.

Shame turned her face crimson. "Oh! Okay. I'm sorry for shouting at you, sir. You're right. I'm not a beach person at all. This trip is a gift. Well, then, see you later. Bye, Mr. Ryan." She blurted out her farewell in a rush to end the uncomfortable encounter, then stepped back and shut the door. *Shitshitshitshitshit!*

Krista thumped her head on the door. "Ugh, how embarrassing," she whispered harshly. "How could I be so unbelievably rude to the boss? I am *so* going to get fired next Monday."

She hurried to the window to watch Mr. Ryan walk back to his cottage, every now and then glancing back over his shoulder at Krista's door with a perplexed look on his face.

Please let him not be angry. She had never shown him hostility, even when they argued about strategies at work. Maybe he was merely puzzled by her irrational behavior. Fingers crossed, she walked to the dining area hoping she was right.

As a thought crossed her mind she halted in her tracks, eyes narrowed with suspicion. A makeover, a fancy resort in Boracay, sexy clothes ... and Mr. Ryan? *Would my barkada really go that far?* Possibly. She wouldn't put it past them to manipulate events to suit their goals, especially with Maddie as the ringleader.

I did say, "Plan for whatever you think I'd need." Shaking her head at her friends' audacity, Krista proceeded to the table. Whether Blake Ryan was part of their plan, or whether it was merely a coincidence he was here at the same time didn't matter. He was very much in it now.

Sitting down to eat her morning snack of the offerings from the fruit basket, she considered her

7

next steps. Mr. Ryan was a complication she had not prepared for.

In all her adult life, no other man had made her the focus of his attention like her boss did. He made her feel self-conscious during meetings they attended together, especially these past couple of months. His eyes were always on her, even when she was not talking or when he should have been watching the presentation.

Krista had to admit, he wasn't the only one looking. Whenever they were in the same room, she would mark the seat reserved for him and choose a chair across and at an angle, so she could watch him discreetly.

It was a pleasure to look at him for he possessed the looks and build of a Hollywood leading man. His face was sculpted rather than chiseled; his body fit, but not overly bulky like a weightlifter's.

He always wore a suit, just like her, but his fit him perfectly. They were probably tailored for him in Hong Kong or Bangkok, while hers were off the rack from SM, the country's largest department store chain. He and those bespoke suits were likely the reason the temperature in their office was in the mid-teens centigrade.

Krista smiled, remembering one of the few conversations she had with the big boss before today. They'd just finished their annual business review and she was putting away the presentation materials when he spoke to her. She hadn't noticed him staying behind.

"Excellent analysis, Ms. Lopez." He always pronounced it "Low-pez", the same as the famous Jennifer, rather than the Filipino way of "Law-pes".

"Thank you, sir. It was a team effort." She kept her head down to hide her flush of pleasure from his compliment.

Beneath her lashes, she tracked his legs. He took several steps forward until he was in front of the table where she was shuffling papers around. Krista thought it was starting to get a little crowded in that space, even though she felt all aflutter by his nearness.

"How do you like working with us so far?"

Courtesy demanded she look at him while he talked to her. A smile played on his mouth—she focused on that. "I'm enjoying it here. It's been stimulating." His lips twitched in amusement, making her realize that her last word could be misinterpreted as flirty. Her eyes flew to his. "Intellectually, I mean."

"Of course. I thought so myself, especially this last quarter." She must have frowned in confusion, because he changed the subject. "You don't find it overly cold?"

If anything, it was too warm. He perched on the table, his slacks stretched tightly over his powerfully built thighs. Her mouth went dry, but she managed to croak out, "The Siberia in Bonifacio Global City?" At his laugh, she relaxed and continued. "No. I'm perfectly comfortable. I'm well—" The rest of her statement was cut off by one of the VPs, who had entered the conference room to

9

speak to Mr. Ryan. She had nodded to him and backed out of the room, relief coursing through her.

Deep inside the memory, Krista stared morosely at the mango peel on her plate. Embarrassingly, she had been about to say something that would draw his attention to her Asian-size-Large body. *Insulated. Padded.* She was going to point to her ill-fitting suit, which covered her from neck to ankle. Another point of frustration her *barkada* shared about her. They liked to call her voluptuous and wanted her to wear clothes that showed off her shape instead of hiding it.

The thought of her friends reminded her of the suspicion about their scheme. Krista couldn't blame them for running out of patience with her. She *had* made a promise to their friend Sheila, who had died in her hometown of Leyte during the Super Typhoon Yolanda.

Krista felt tightness in her chest as grief coursed through her. Sheila, too, had gone on a one-week vacation from work during the All Saints' Day break of 2013. She was in Leyte on the 8th of November, unaware that the storm would wipe out almost everything in its path—including Sheila herself.

The girls held a memorial for her when it was confirmed she had died a heroine who saved her nephew from drowning. They all swore they would live their lives to the fullest each day, pledging to never put off plans and dreams for tomorrow. And they all promised to carry out a monumental act on their thirtieth birthday, to do the things Sheila had delayed accomplishing, to celebrate reaching the milestone their friend had never attained. They called it the Turning-Thirty Vow.

Krista's four friends had already fulfilled their sworn promises, either by design or by accident. Lisa's first child was born on her birthday; Jenny married her longtime boyfriend on hers; in September, Angela left her dead-end job, started her own company, and went skydiving; and last week, Maddie received a huge promotion and a flashy new car as thirtieth birthday gifts.

Her own milestone day would be in the middle of this week, on November 2nd, but she couldn't hope to match most of her friends' Turning-Thirty feats. They jokingly called her an NBSB—No Boyfriend Since Birth—so no wedding and no baby for her. She started her new job in May, and so far, she liked it. She would not be quitting anytime soon. Nor would she be getting a promotion, since her probationary period just ended last Friday.

She was the only one who hadn't been enjoying everything life had to offer each day. Nothing in Krista's life changed after they'd made the vow, nor since they'd all left college. Work, work, and more work. It was all she did. She had obtained her MBA purely for her career advancement and financial security. It wasn't a case of taking advantage of an opportunity that suddenly came her way. *There was no impulse there. No seizing the moment.*

"I have become like Sheila." Krista shuddered, suddenly feeling cold. *I also want to go*

11

somewhere I haven't been, do things I haven't done, and fall in love with someone who treats me like an equal. Despite her promises to her friends and herself, she kept putting off her goals until she turned thirty. She experienced a pang of regret for all the times she'd declined Angela's invitations to try new adventures with her. She was sorry for snapping at Maddie whenever her friend tried to fix her up on a date.

In truth, all of them attempted to set her up with someone in the fourteen years they had known each other. But after a couple of awful blind-date experiences, she began to make excuses for not going. Her reasons were legitimate at the time, but looking back at things now, perhaps she could have made an exception a time or two. Krista had a fantastic expectation that she would know right away when she finally fell in love. She hadn't anticipated reaching thirty without feeling an attraction towards any man.

Well, Krista, thirty is barreling around the corner; it's time to meet it headlong. And correction, there is a man you are attracted to—Mr. Blake Ryan.

Her eyes widened as inspiration struck. *That's it! There's an opportunity right now, right here in Boracay, and I'm going to take it.*

Adrenaline rushing through her, Krista jumped up and strode to the bedroom to pick out one of her new bikini sets. She removed her boring old clothes and put on the daring attire. Again, she let her hair down and took off her glasses—she only required them for reading and to complete the nerdy look she'd been trying to project. They weren't necessary now, especially with her newly conceived plans.

Krista smiled with a glint in her eyes at the "new her" in the mirror. With the application of mascara and shimmery lip gloss—also helpfully provided by her friends—her excitement gave her cheeks a natural blush. No more dowdiness. Except for her pale skin, she looked like she could fit in, here in Boracay. *I just may be able to pull this off.*

"They want something special, huh? I'll give them something extraordinary, indeed. It must start with an apology to Mr. Blake Ryan. He is essential to accomplishing my Turning-Thirty Vow."

Chapter Two

Boracay [bo-rock-eye], n. – a small island in the
Philippines (located approximately 315 km (196 mi)
south of Manila and 2 km off the northwest tip of
Panay Island).

The resort—simply called Perlas after "Pearl of the
Orient Seas," the romantic moniker for the
Philippines—was nestled on the northeast area of
Boracay Island. The whole western side, with its
world famous White Beach, was the well-developed
and most-visited part. Since the 1990s, several
international travel publications and agencies had
showered the island with awards and accolades,
attracting the tourists in droves.

 The objective of Blake and the other owners
of Perlas was to provide the rich and famous with the
Boracay experience while maintaining their privacy.
If they chose to party with the crowds in White
Beach, guests could avail themselves of a motorboat
for trips to and from their destination at their
convenience. If they preferred to stay, the resort
promised to deliver everything a discerning traveler
needed at the touch of a button.

 It had taken his friends three years to convince
Blake to partner with them to build this property, but
when he committed to the venture, he was all in.
Boracay was his favorite place in the Philippines.
He'd visited at least once a year since he moved from
the US.

He had stayed at various parts of the island but found each of his accommodations lacking. The Shangri-La came close to his ideal, except it was much too big, and the presence of children inhibited his pleasure. He had nothing against kids—he hoped to have one or two someday, but that day hadn't arrived yet.

At thirty-three, Blake still enjoyed his bachelor status. Living in the Philippines worked well for him. It allowed him to be far away from his mother's nagging, or as she called it, "loving pressure," to get married and produce grandchildren for her and his dad.

His two brothers obviously agreed with him; they also left New York as soon as they could. Southeast Asia seemed to hold a special attraction for the Ryan brothers. Aidan was based in Singapore, and Craig worked in Koh Samui, Thailand. Only the baby in the family, their sister Darcy, stayed in the US with their parents. As he left his cottage to take the short path to the beach, Blake made a mental note to invite his brothers to Perlas during Christmas break.

An adult-only resort, Perlas had a limited occupancy of sixty. There were ten cottages—called *kubo*, after the traditional Filipino thatched palm hut—and twenty suites, or *silid*—bedroom in the vernacular. The cottages all had restricted beach access, while each of the suites in the main building boasted of ocean views.

At the end of the path, Blake stopped for a moment to take in the beauty of his surroundings. He curled his toes into the powdery, white sand and breathed the sweet-smelling morning air. With an appreciative look at the cloudless blue sky, he broke into a run and dove into the clear aquamarine waters of the Sibuyan Sea.

In Makati, the country's central business district where he worked and lived, Blake made it a point to swim daily in his condominium's rooftop pool. *Nothing can beat the sun-warmed seawaters of the islands, though. I'll take it over heavily chlorinated pool water, any day.*

After several rigorous laps from the shore to one of the buoys, Blake turned to float on his back. His thoughts turned to the intriguing woman who captured his attention the moment he interviewed her.

Her direct-to-the-point manner had appealed to him greatly, more so than the fawning style of the other applicants. He'd hired her on the spot and had never regretted his decision.

Krista Lopez, his senior market analyst, was one feisty lady. She was a welcome departure from her demure and timid compatriots. In the six months since she joined the company, Krista had proven herself to him and to the board of directors. She had been invaluable with her keen insight during the September fiscal year review. He was sure no one would object if he promoted her to the management team at the end of her first year.

Tired of floating, Blake climbed onto one of the resort's several platforms for water sports staging, placed at several intervals in the middle of the sea. He checked that he was out of sight, then took off his swim shorts to work on his overall tan. He lay face down with his shorts between his privates and the rough wooden boards. Pillowing his head on his arms, he continued to contemplate the estimable Ms. Lopez.

Since she reported to someone further down in the company's management, Blake didn't see her every day at the office. During the monthly general meetings, and whenever their service partners had major presentations that required his presence, his admiration continued to grow.

Despite the schoolmarm outfits and simple makeup, she carried herself gracefully. She always sat tall, and her walk was a sight to behold. The woman glided across the room, not merely walked. "Glided? Really?" Blake grinned at the poetic turn his musings had taken. He turned over. His back was starting to prickle from the sun exposure.

A slight smile appeared on his face as he recalled the first time he sat beside her during a briefing, two months ago. She wore her usual pantsuit, but on her feet were sexy fire-engine-red heels. When she stood no one could see her shoes because her pants were wide-legged and fell almost to the floor. While seated with one of her crossed legs swinging to a silent beat only she could hear, the shoes were eye-catching to say the least.

Since then, he had speculated on what else Ms. Krista Lopez might be hiding beneath her unflattering outfits and stern librarian demeanor. That memorable day was probably when he decided he wanted her.

Shortly after, Blake sought to know more about her; he hit the jackpot when he learned of

Krista's close friendship with Madeleine Duvall. Madeleine, or Maddie as she liked to be called, was a part-French, part-Filipina public relations dynamo. Both his company and Perlas engaged her agency's services for PR and events management.

He and Maddie moved in the same circles with their common interests. They had dated a couple of times before they started working together, but found no sparks of mutual attraction. Their casual attitude towards relationships was too similar, and they agreed to keep their relationship casually professional.

The connection between the two women fascinated him. Maddie's claim that they'd become friends at first sight surprised Blake. Yes, they were both intelligent, of the same age, and had similar multi-ethnic backgrounds. But in personal style and behavior they were miles apart.

Maddie was overtly sensual, likely a byproduct of her bohemian upbringing. In contrast, Krista maintained a controlled and old-fashioned conservatism, which suggested a strict Catholic rearing. Blake once again grinned at the memory of Krista's red shoes. *Plenty of Catholic girls have a rebellious streak in them; perhaps I can bring out the bad girl in Krista.* He laughed out loud at the thought. He did love a good challenge.

Blake had lied to Krista when he knocked on her door. He knew it was really her. The idea to get Krista here in Boracay was his, even though he suspected she was not a beach person. He wanted her here because he was coming to the island himself.

When Maddie casually mentioned that she and some friends were conspiring to give Krista the vacation of a lifetime, he suggested Perlas. She gave him a raised eyebrow and a warning look, but agreed readily enough. He figured she had her own agenda, and using him served her purposes.

Blake was only too happy to take advantage of the opportunity to get closer to one Ms. Krista Lopez. He maneuvered the cottage assignment to place hers beside his, which for the past year had been his privilege as an owner.

He had a firm policy against dating a colleague; it was a rule he intended to break for an extraordinarily special woman. This week was his lucky chance. It was now or never.

Blake ended his pondering with that thought. He put on his shorts and dove back into the sea. Undaunted by Krista's negative reception earlier, he headed for the first step in his planned seduction—an invitation to dinner tonight.

His sudden appearance had probably rattled her, making her feel unsure. She'd lashed out. He had seen her blushes whenever they got close; he was sure he'd sparked her interest, too. *Does she think I haven't noticed how she makes it a point to keep her distance from me? Not a chance.*

Reaching the shore, Blake's jaw dropped as a goddess walked gracefully towards him. The vision before him was clad in a black bikini top that barely contained her generous breasts. Her round hips were wrapped in a black-and-white, vertically striped sarong. She held a pair of jeweled sandals in one hand. Her wavy, shoulder-length hair, lifted by the gentle breeze, blew into her pretty face. She brushed it away with her free hand. *Wow! It's Krista.*

The stirring of arousal filled him, but Blake tried to clamp down on it. It wouldn't do to overwhelm her with his sexual pursuit so soon. "Think of profit margins and returns on investments," he advised himself. His wet swimsuit aided in cooling his ardor as he continued to admire the transformed image of the woman who had been occupying his thoughts for the past two months.

This new Krista—this stunning beauty who came to a sudden stop upon seeing him—was straight out of his most erotic dreams.

"Mr. Ryan," Krista began as he got closer.

"Blake, please. May I call you Krista?"

"Of course, sir ... I mean ... Blake. I would like to apologize again about my outburst earlier. My flight was quite early, and I didn't get enough sleep last night." Krista fidgeted with the ties of her sarong as she spoke, which drew his eyes to her shapely waist.

"And I would like to express my regret one more time for barging in on you so early, and for making you think I question your suitability to the beach."

He dragged his eyes back to her blushing face. "I was delighted to see a familiar face; it didn't occur to me you might be less than enthusiastic to meet someone from work during your holiday." His voice held a teasing tone. Gesturing for her to resume her walk, he fell in step with her, matching his stride to her shorter steps.

"I have to admit I was a bit *hangry*, too," Krista confessed sheepishly.

"*Hangry?*"

"You know, the unprovoked rage usually experienced by people who skipped a meal," she clarified with a lilting laugh. He joined in her merriment; he liked her newly relaxed mood.

"Plus, I was a little resentful I had to work overtime last week because you had to go on your vacation." She said this with a raised eyebrow, the glint in her eyes suggesting playfulness.

He raised his own eyebrow in response. "So, the truth comes out. But didn't you consider that all your overtime was to prepare for your own vacation? It's a weeklong break. I only gave the employees the Monday off because the holidays were in the middle of the week. You're on leave Thursday and Friday, too."

She stopped walking and faced him with her hands clasped in front of her chest. "You personally approved my two extra days of vacation leave? Oh, thank you for not keeping me chained to my desk, Mr. Generous-And-Not-A-Total-Slave-Driver CEO. Thank you very much!" She fluttered her eyelashes overdramatically.

He burst out laughing at her sass. "You're welcome, Ms. Krista Middle-Name-Sarcastic Lopez." They stood there grinning at each other, the earlier misunderstanding forgiven and forgotten.

This is good. She was starting to feel comfortable with him. At the office, he cultivated an aloof attitude around the female staff. On the island, especially around Krista, he wanted to be warm and approachable.

She resumed her walk, her gaze on the sea. "Seriously, I could really use the break. I haven't had a holiday since I started my master's degree, two years ago. I was working the whole time and then when I finished my MBA, I joined your corporation right away. But don't tell my friends I admitted that, because they would be all smug and say, 'We told you so!'" She grinned, affection for her squad obvious in her voice.

Taking advantage of the marked change in her attitude towards him, Blake suggested, "Would you like to grab some lunch? I just had a long swim, and I'm famished. I may get *hangry*, too, if I don't eat soon."

She stopped and peered up at him, pondering the invitation. He kept a relaxed smile on his face, but inside he was willing her to agree.

"Sure." She looked around. "But where?" They had come to the end of the beach, close to the cliffs.

Blake pointed to a path on the right. "That leads to my kubo. We can call in an order for the kitchen to bring food down, and we can eat at the cabana in the garden. I also need to shower and change clothes." He gestured to his chest and arms, where the salt had started to crystallize on his bronzed skin.

Krista stared at his chest for a beat too long, as if mesmerized by the sight, then turned towards his cottage. A blush bloomed again on her cheeks. After a shaky breath, she looked up at him and said, "Okay."

Satisfied he was getting his way, he sought to reassure her. "Don't look so scared. I don't eat senior market analysts for lunch." *Is she relieved or disappointed? I can't tell.* He continued cheekily, "Maybe for dinner, but not for lunch." He winked at her, only half joking.

She colored more at his teasing but squared her shoulders and glided forward. He motioned for her to precede him onto the path so he could watch her from behind. He was going to need a cold shower to dampen his libido; the sight of her round bottom bouncing as she walked made him randy again.

Since fixing his eyes on her two months ago, Blake had been celibate. He was tired of dealing with Makati's devious single ladies, especially those who deliberately pursued Western expatriates like him, to have a perceived better life elsewhere.

The Filipinas were known to be among the most beautiful women in the world, but since he became a resident of the country, Blake made sure to conduct his bedroom affairs discreetly, with sophisticated expats or transient visitors instead.

These days, he preferred to keep company with his buddies or with platonic female friends like Maddie. His appetite for meaningless liaisons had left him.

Blake jogged past her to open his door. He picked up a menu from the kitchen counter and handed it to her. "Can you order for us? I'll have the chicken and pork *adobo*, *chop suey*, and ripe mango shake. Thanks!"

He strode briskly towards his bedroom, fully aware of her irate gaze on his back. He had glimpsed a flash of temper on her face when he issued the order. In truth, his skin had started to itch, but his rush to get away was mainly to hide his growing erection from her.

Chapter Three

Sarap [sa-rap], adj. – delicious.

Krista stared at Blake's back in dumbfounded silence. *What an arrogant ass!* She had to admit, he was drop-dead gorgeous and mouth-wateringly sexy, but still arrogant and still an ass. *Ordering me about like I work for him.* She slapped a hand on her forehead. *Oh, wait. I do work for him. He's lucky I'm hungry or I'd walk out on his fine ass.*

With a huff, she moved to sit on the plush sofa. Taking the cottage phone in hand, she dialed room service and gave his selections along with her pork *sinigang*, deep-fried whole tilapia, and *buko* juice. She asked for three servings of rice, guessing he could probably polish those off with no problem at all.

Her task accomplished, Krista surveyed the luxurious accommodations. His *kubo* was like hers, just bigger. It had all the necessary elements of a house—living room, dining room, kitchen, bedroom, and bathroom. It was probably twice the size of her apartment in Makati.

Correction, it was three times as big as her unit. Her kubo was the one that could fit two of her city home. The only resemblances this structure had to a traditional nipa hut were the thatched roof covering the building and the wooden support and beams. Everything else was modern and fancy, from the central air-conditioning system to the sleek appliances and high-tech glass windows.

Mutya, the Perlas hostess who brought her down to her cottage in a golf cart, had taken the scenic route and showed her around the resort. She pointed to this as the Maharlika Kubo where the owners usually stayed when they were in Boracay. *The Royal Hut? Is Blake one of the partners of Perlas?* She had to ask Maddie. Or better yet, she would ask the man himself later, during lunch.

Tucking her bare feet under her legs, Krista leaned back on the sofa and thought about her brilliant idea for the something extraordinary she would do for her thirtieth birthday.

Given that she was in a private island paradise with a super-sexy guy who was also turned on by her—*yep, saw that bulge in his shorts*—it didn't require a genius to guess her decision. She would give in to the attraction between herself and Blake. She was going to allow Mr. CEO to seduce her into giving him her virginity.

Krista puffed out a deep breath. She knew her generous curves could incite lust in men. Hadn't she endured inappropriate groping from her two previous blind dates because of her shape? She didn't know what triggered her boss's interest in her before, but his obvious physical response to her bikini-clad body was enough proof that her plan could work.

As he didn't strike her as someone who wanted a long-term relationship, she was sure Blake would agree to a secret, no-strings-attached affair for one week. They could go back to simply being Mr.

Ryan and Ms. Lopez when they returned to the city. *Perhaps what happens in Boracay can stay in Boracay.*

Nanay is going to freak out if she finds out. She brushed away the unwelcome thought. Her mother's fears about Krista following in her footsteps had been the main reason Krista got fat, covered up her fair skin, and made herself unattractive. *What she doesn't know won't hurt her.*

While changing into the bikini, Krista had fully embraced the made-over version of herself that her friends aided in creating. After nearly thirty years of being an obedient daughter, responsible older sister, diligent student, steady worker, and supportive friend, now was the time to just be her. If being herself meant finally giving in to her repressed sensuality, so be it.

When she removed her glasses, let her hair down, and donned her itty-bitty bikini to go for her walk at the beach, Krista had literally shed the persona she'd worn since leaving college—that of a novice on her way to the nunnery. She smiled at how apt the comparison was. For too long she had undertaken the vows of poverty, chastity, and obedience; not by choice, but by necessity.

No more, she promised herself. *No more playing down my looks. No more shying away from romance. None of that Little Miss Planner shtick.*

Not so little. She smirked, but she'd go with it. From now on, she would heed the line from a poem by Robert Herrick that was in one of her favorite movies, *Dead Poets' Society*: "Gather ye rosebuds while ye may." She giggled at how fitting the poem's title was: "To the Virgins, to Make Much of Time."

Speaking of virgins, the person taking an inordinate amount of time in the shower was definitely not one. Krista had almost fallen flat on her face when she saw him emerge from the water. *Whoa! Mr. Blake Ryan is hot!* She knew he was immensely attractive in his suits, but shirtless he was sexy with a sizzling capital S.

He resembled the actor who played Superman in the movies, with similar curly black hair, blue eyes, and a dimple on his chin. The exception was her boss's nose. It was slightly crooked, as if it had been broken in the past. And the body, *hmm*, the body was also like the actor's, with well-muscled thighs, sculpted abs, and a golden chest sprinkled with dark hair that tapered into his swim shorts. Of course she drooled. She was only human, after all.

A knock on the cottage's front door signaled the end of her daydreams. The food had arrived.

Putting on her sandals, she rushed to let the servers in. She led them outside to set up in the cabana by the pool. *It might be rude, but if Blake isn't out in five minutes, I'll start eating without him. He's been in the shower for thirty minutes already. What could be taking so long? I can wash my hair faster than that.*

***

The cold shower wasn't working. Blake leaned back on the marbled tiles of the shower enclosure and took his swollen cock in hand. Imagining Krista's pouty lips opening wide and taking his length into her mouth made him harden more. He pictured himself filling his hands with her full breasts while she sucked him, and that was all it took to make him blow his load on the walls of the shower. *Pathetic!*

He turned the knob to change the spray to warm and rinsed off, scolding himself for going off like a teenager with his first girl. He hadn't resorted to giving himself a hand job since he was in high school. *This seduction better be quick, otherwise I might develop carpal tunnel syndrome.*

Stepping out of the shower, he reached for the towel to dry himself. Krista's blushes and the way she stared at his chest suggested there was a reciprocal attraction there. He just had to fan the flames, and they would burn up the sheets soon enough.

After donning another t-shirt-and-shorts ensemble—his uniform whenever he was at the island—Blake left the bedroom to join Krista in the garden. He paused by the door feeling a twinge of disappointment when he saw she had rearranged her sarong to fashion it into a halter dress that covered her whole torso and upper legs. On second thought, maybe it was better not to get aroused while eating lunch.

He approached on bare feet. As he got closer, he was alarmed by her pose—elbow on the table, chin propped in her hand, and mouth turned down at the corners. "Is anything wrong?"

She dropped her hand to the table. "I didn't bring money with me, so I couldn't give the waiters a tip." The oversight clearly distressed her.

He sat across from her, relieved that it was nothing serious. "Don't worry about it. The office will put the charge on my account, and I'll make sure the staff is compensated."

Blake was impressed by Krista's thoughtful consideration of the waitstaff. Many people deemed those in the service industry to be of lower class. None of his former dates were as kind.

"Be that as it may, I still feel guilty. I got their names. I hope to see them again at dinner or some other time during the week, so I can make it up to them."

"I'm sure they'll appreciate it. Come on, let's eat," he invited, lifting the covers off the platters and immediately digging into his lunch.

He had taken a liking to Filipino food, finding it tasty and flavorful. Well, except for *balut*, the fertilized duck embryo the locals ate direct from the shell. *Yuck.* The chicken and pork *adobo*—the Philippines' unofficial national dish—was one of his favorites, along with the roasted pig *lechon* and stir-fried rice noodles *pancit bihon*.

Krista tucked into her meal with gusto, leaving Blake enthralled by the way she puckered her lips after taking a sip of the broth from her sour *sinigang* soup. He had to mentally shake himself to pay attention to his own food.

"Hmm, *sarap*!" The garlic saltiness of the adobo sauce and the perfect tenderness of the meat hit his taste buds and made him groan in satisfaction.

"You can speak *Tagalog*?" Krista referred to the most commonly spoken language in Metro Manila.

"*Konti lang.* Only a little. I know enough to order food, greet people, not get lost when I travel, and to know when somebody is talking about me." He joked, "*Hindi ako pwedeng ibenta.*" No one could sell him out.

She laughed at his jest. "*Galing!* How long have you been here?"

"Five years last July. I was supposed to stay for three years, but I fell in love with the country and the people, and I decided to extend my contract. The Philippine office has the hardest-working employees in the whole company. And the most beautiful women in the world are here," he declared, pointing at her with his spoon. He had learned early on to eat with spoon and fork instead of the American fork-and-knife combination.

"That's a long time. How come you haven't married any of these beautiful Filipinas you mentioned?" she teased, her eyes on his ringless left hand. She paused in her eating and leaned back, awaiting his response.

He put down his utensils and mimicked her pose. "The honest answer is I wasn't ready. It's a cliché to be sure, but I've been enjoying the lifestyle of the single, unencumbered bachelor so much, I was reluctant to give it up." *That's been true in the past. Who knows what tomorrow will bring.*

"What about you? How come you're not Mrs. Somebody yet?" Of course, he knew she was single from Maddie. It couldn't hurt to hear it directly from Krista. He also wanted to find out her relationship history.

She picked up her coconut juice in a half-shell and after a fortifying sip, rejoined, "No one has ever asked." She fiddled with her straw and looked everywhere but at him.

No one? As in she's never had a boyfriend? "No way! Are these Pinoy men so blind that they can't see the treasure you are? You're remarkably attractive, exceptionally smart, and very sexy."

"Yes way!" She grinned at his outburst. "Too tall, too clever, and before today, too frumpy—yep, that's me." She crossed her arms over her chest and challenged him. "Don't tell me you actually liked my boxy pantsuits. I won't believe you."

"No, but seeing you out of them made it all worthwhile in the end," he retorted, revealing his desire for her in his heated gaze. *Step one, done. Time for step two.*

Chapter Four

Halik [ha-leek], n. – kiss.

"Oh." Krista uncrossed her arms and reached for a glass of water, her mouth suddenly dry at hearing those provocative words. She jolted when instead of the cool glass, her hand brushed against warm flesh. Blake's hand captured hers. He drew circles in the middle of her palm with his thumb, sending her pulse skittering.

There it is! She had only felt that electricity a few times, each instance generated by him. It first happened when they shook hands after she got the job. The next time, he had unexpectedly joined a meeting and sat close—much too close—beside her. The last time was this morning when he appeared on her doorstep.

In all those encounters she had recoiled, retreated like the coward she was. This time she would not draw back. She would face this connection head on. Krista raised her chin and met his gaze, letting him see her acquiescence.

Without releasing her hand, Blake stood up and pulled her to her feet. "Krista, you must know that I'm attracted to you. And I think—check that—I am certain you feel the same way about me. Our chemistry is off the charts. What do you say we explore this thing between us while we're here in Boracay, and see where it leads?" He cupped her face tenderly and lightly pressed his thumb over her lower lip. His blue eyes darkened with desire.

"Blake, I … I want that, too. But I have a confession to make," she said huskily. "I've never done this." It was important to be honest with him about her inexperience. If it was going to turn him off, she needed to know before they went any further.

Braced for disappointment, she still felt a sense of loss when he removed his hand from her face. Only to shiver a heartbeat later when he raised her arms to rest on his shoulders.

"Never done what, sweetheart?" One of his hands played lightly with her hair while the other rested at the small of her back. He pulled her close until her suddenly tight nipples touched his shirt-clad chest. His touch was feather light but firm.

"All of it. I've never been kissed. Never been touched," she whispered.

If it was possible, his gaze heated more at her confession of innocence.

"Well, Krista, darling," he said seductively as he drew her closer in his embrace, "I hope you're a good student, because I will teach you all you need to know about kissing and about touching."

Her eyes closed at the unfamiliar feelings that bombarded her senses. Mixed in was relief. He was not repelled. He still wanted her.

"Open your eyes, love. I want you to never forget who gave you your first kiss, or touched you for the first time," he commanded gently. With heavy lids she opened her eyes, then widened them in confusion when his head came down and his lips landed on her forehead.

He let out a laugh at the disappointed expression on her face. "Relax, sweetheart," he kissed the tip of her nose, then both cheeks. "This won't hurt," he whispered in her ear. "You may even like it."

Gentle as the breeze that wafted in the early afternoon air, his kiss at the curve of her neck made her shiver in response. Then, after a seemingly endless pause, he finally touched his lips to hers.

The kiss was soft at first, his lips tracing the shape of her mouth as if he was committing it to memory. *And warm, oh so warm.* Then, with his tongue seeking entry, and the hand caressing her face aiding in his request to let him in, she yielded and opened her mouth. She felt the heat slam into her whole being. She couldn't help herself; she had to disobey him and close her eyes. The sensations overwhelmed her.

Tightening her hold on him, she boldly touched her tongue to his. He groaned and deepened the kiss, his tongue tangling with hers. Her breasts plumped up more, her nipples distended. Down below, dampness seeped through her bikini bottoms.

She lowered her arms from his neck, intending to lift his shirt so she could touch him, but his hands stopped her. He broke off the kiss, raised their joined hands to his chest, and rested his forehead on hers. He was breathing heavily.

Swaying on her feet, Krista asked in bewilderment, "Why did you stop?"

"Baby, if we don't stop right now, I'll carry you back inside and we'll be doing more than what you're ready for." He moved his hips against her stomach, making her feel the hardness between his thighs. "Make no mistake, I want to make love to you. I want to kiss you all over and worship you from the top of your head to the bottom of your feet. But you have to be ready, and although it kills me to say this, I don't think you are."

God. Why does he have to be so honorable? And so right? Damn it. It was only a couple of hours ago that she'd decided on this course of action. She was truly taking to heart this seizing the moment motto.

Krista took a deep breath, then gently withdrew from his hold. Thankful that her weak knees held firm, she regarded him. He wasn't lying. The veins on his neck stood out, and his muscles were rigid. He was really keeping a tight rein on his self-control.

Looking up at him, she admitted, "You're right, Blake. I'm not ready right now. It's too soon. Too fast." He nodded, appearing regretful. "Like I said, I'm open to exploring our attraction to each other while we're here in Boracay. I agree with you about our chemistry." She paused to gauge his reaction.

"And that's why this morning, I decided to give up my virginity." His eyes grew huge. "I'm giving it to you." She shook her head when he started to speak. "But, not yet, not right this minute."

"Sometime this week, hopefully?" His tone was light, teasing.

"Maybe." She smiled at him. "Maybe not." She laughed when he groaned.

Stepping back to evade him as he looked about to take her back in his arms, she bumped into the table and saw the remnants of their lunch. Looking for a distraction, Krista started clearing up the dishes.

"Just leave them there. I'll call the staff to take them away later." At her sudden frown, he declared, "If I promise to double their tip to make up for not getting one earlier, will you stop cleaning up, please?" He drew out the last word in exasperation.

His aggrieved tone made her grin. "You, Mr. Ryan, are lazy."

"Darn right I am!" he proudly proclaimed. They both laughed at the untruthful boast. "What are your plans for this afternoon?"

"I want a nap. All that glorious food is making me sleepy. I should also check in with my family and friends. They might think I'm at the bottom of the ocean right now, since I haven't called to tell them I arrived safely." She bent to pick up her sandals from under the table where she had kicked them during lunch. When she straightened, she caught him staring at her butt, an arrested look on his face. She reached up to kiss his cheek, surprising herself with how comfortable she felt, showing him physical affection. "Thanks for lunch. Will I see you at dinner?"

"Yes, I'll knock on your door at five thirty, and we'll take a short tour around the resort before we eat. It's seafood-feast night. Bring your appetite."

"You know it. I love seafood," she enthused. Krista turned towards the path and trilled, "See you later, alligator!"

"After a while, crocodile," he quipped right back, smiling.

***

Blake stared absently at the space she had occupied, the echo of her laughter still ringing in his ears. *Holy crap, a virgin!* He pulled up a chair and plunked himself down. Everything he knew about Krista pointed to her inexperience. Still, the confirmation staggered him. *Have I ever found a virgin this desirable?* He didn't have to think hard. *Never.* He had purposely avoided them.

He removed his shirt and leaned back on the chair, chuckling at how Krista's allegation of his laziness was proven true. In his defense, he was on vacation, and wasn't the whole point of it to rest and relax?

Blake had lost his own virginity at sixteen to his older brother's high school girlfriend. Summer, the Broadway-star-wannabe, had wanted to make Aidan jealous. Angry at his plan to join the Air Force after graduation, she'd arranged to have him find her in Blake's room, to teach Aidan a lesson on how he'd be losing out. It didn't work; even at seventeen, the oldest Ryan son could be a right bastard whenever he chose. Aidan was mildly amused at finding them together. He broke up with her right there and then.

Since that incident, his brother often teased him that he planned to delay his "discovery" until Blake had his orgasm, only to realize he didn't have long to wait. Five-Minute-Blake was his nickname for a while in the Ryan household, much to his dismay.

It was a lifetime ago, but Blake was grateful to Aidan's ex for initiating him into the carnal world.

He loved the feeling of a soft body beneath him; he anticipated hearing the moans from a woman's throat. The experience of his heartbeat matching the cadence of his thrusts was something he looked forward to. Best of all, he absolutely adored the explosion at the end—hers and his, as their climaxes hit them.

Since the first fumbling attempt with Summer, he always ensured that his partners found satisfaction before he did. *I plain love sex, that's God's honest truth.*

Blake moved to recline on a sunbed, sprawling his long body onto it with a contented sigh. One of his many contributions to the resort had been making sure the furniture fit Western dimensions, especially the beds in the cottages. Too many resorts in Asia had undersized furnishings, uncomfortable for a man of his proportions.

He yawned and recalled Krista's suggestion of a nap.

Ah, Krista. She was never far from his thoughts. Since seeing her curvy body revealed, he was even more drawn to her. Back in Makati, he had been waiting for the perfect opportunity to discreetly ask her out. He didn't want to do it while they were at work; it would have seemed unprofessional. He sought a social situation, away from the office, to show his interest in her was purely personal. But they never had any such encounters. They lived in different parts of the city and never bumped into each other. Now he had Krista exactly where he wanted her—beside him and away from the prying eyes of the people in the office.

God, she was exquisite. He loved how their bodies aligned, how their heights made them fit together just right. It was all he could do to keep his hands still on her waist. His palms itched to cup her curvy ass, plump her luscious breasts even more. He bet they would spill over his hands, the way they did from her bikini top. He longed to divest her of those tiny triangle-shaped bits of cloth and take her hard nipples in his mouth. Blake rubbed his chest, remembering how the stiff peaks had brushed against his body during their kiss.

Their kiss. Her first kiss. Ever. It was often said that a girl never forgets her first kiss. He knew he would always remember the pure, unadulterated pleasure of their lips touching for the first time.

He grinned, thinking about the adorable expression on her face when he pulled her closer. She had tightly shut both her eyes and mouth as if she were preparing for a surprise, unsure whether she would like it. The disappointment that crossed her features when he kissed her on the forehead pleased him to no end. So did her body's response when he finally brought his wandering lips to hers. She might have been an innocent, but she seemed eagerly receptive to the delights of the flesh.

The fragrant perfume of her skin, her throaty moans, and the way she met his searching tongue with bold forays of her own all inflamed him. *Oh yes, that was a kiss to remember for sure.*

His cock definitely had not forgotten. Nearly crazy with the desire to ravish her, he had forced himself to slow down and savor her intoxicating sweetness. Blake grimaced as he adjusted his shorts over his tight and aching member. *Not this again.* He hoped she wouldn't make him wait very long, otherwise he would suffer from blue balls. Add that to his carpal tunnel and he'd be crippled before long.

Well, at least for today, he had only himself to blame for halting their lovemaking. His sudden development of scruples surprised even Blake. *Since when did I become a bloody Boy Scout, turning a hot, willing woman away from my bed?*

Blake rose from the sunbed and shrugged his shirt back on. It was time to call the staff, to give them the promised tip.

On his way into his kubo, he paused to look in the direction of Krista's cottage. He vowed that when he finally got her to a bed, she would be under him, or on top of him, or beside him for a long, long time. *I might let her up for meals, but that's it.* He smirked as he made the ridiculous pledge.

Chapter Five

Yehey [ye-hay] int. – an expression of delight, excitement.

Krista was not at all surprised by the six missed calls on her cellphone. She'd left it in her kubo to regain power, since its battery was drained; she'd forgotten to charge it overnight.

After listening to her voice mail, she sent a text message to her siblings to tell them not to worry. She was still alive. She also texted her friends a short note—*Vid call in 5.* Everyone had a smartphone, so they could all accept a video call at a moment's notice, unless they were driving. All replied with an *ok*. She looked forward to chatting with her friends and sharing her plans. *Or, my agreement with theirs.*

Krista set her laptop on top of the desk in the bedroom and connected to the resort's Wi-Fi. She opened the video conferencing application and started a *M'amie* group call.

Maddie, Jenny, Lisa, Sheila, Angela, and Krista met when they took French as their language elective at the University of the Philippines. They came together as a team for a class presentation and used the group name *M'amie*—short for *mon amie,* a French endearment, which literally meant "my female friend" but also stood for "my dear" or "my love."

Years after their graduation from college and still close friends, they kept the group name. It didn't matter that only Maddie and Angela continued with their study of the romantic language. Sheila's death and their agreed-upon vow only strengthened their bond and made them hold on to one another that much tighter.

In marked contrast with her high school years when she was called a "half-breed," her time spent in college were some of the best of her life. It was in the university, in the company of *M'amie,* that she found acceptance for who she was. Their lack of judgment was one of the reasons these women would be her friends forever.

Krista stayed out of the webcam's range until all the girls showed up on-screen, observing them as they appeared and marveling at how such a disparate group of women had become friends. The always restless Angela was first as usual, followed by the exuberant Jenny, Zen Lisa, and finally, also as usual, the sophisticated Maddie. Krista grinned when Jenny grumbled, "Where the hell is she?"

"Ta da!" Krista jumped in front of the camera, showing off her sarong-clad body. The girls shrieked in surprise and dissolved into boisterous laughter when they saw her preening and doing jazz hands.

"Take it off! Take it off!" Lisa chanted, egging her on to remove her cover-up. When she reached for the tie of the sarong at the back of her neck, Jenny started singing to the beat of the stripper song. "Tana-nanana. Tan-tana. Tan-tana!" Krista kicked her legs in the air, mimicking the can-can dance as she took off the improvised dress.

"Woot-woot!" The girls let out catcalls when she revealed the skimpy black bikini underneath.

Their hilarity continued as dainty-looking Angela Lim put her fingers in her mouth and let out a couple of wolf-whistles.

"Guys, *tama na!* Stop. I'm going to pee in my pants if we keep laughing our heads off." Retying her sarong, Krista shushed the girls and pulled up a chair to sit in front of the computer.

"So, you're not mad at us for packing your suitcase with sexy stuff?" Angela queried.

"I was this morning when I saw them, but since I have nothing else to wear, I decided there's no use getting angry over something I can't change," Krista replied. "I mean, I could hardly wear my soiled clothes every day, could I? Or go naked. I don't think Perlas is that kind of resort," she added with a snort. "Plus, I know they are outrageously expensive, so I can't throw them away. *Sayang.* That would be a waste." She had always been frugal and practical; needed to be for so long.

"Wow! Who are you and what did you do with our friend *Manang* Krista?" Lisa joked, referring to the nickname they had given her ultra-conservative and prim self.

Krista laughed. "She's gone. Erase her from your memory, ladies, because I'm turning over a new leaf. I have finally decided to fulfill my Turning-Thirty Vow. I'm going to copy Gie," she pointed to Angela, "and take *carpe diem* as my new motto. At long last, I'm going to abide by our promise to Sheila to live our lives to the fullest, each and every day." Raising her arms in the air she declared, "Life begins at thirty!"

44

"All right!" Angela cheered.

"*Yehey!*" Jenny and Lisa echoed.

"*Alléluia!*" Maddie responded with an exaggerated eye roll. "And when will this new beginning start? Your birthday isn't until Wednesday. That's four more days," she pressed, raising a perfectly-groomed eyebrow.

Color bloomed in Krista's cheeks, and her lips tingled as the feeling of Blake's kiss came back to her. "Actually, life began today already." She touched her lips with a finger before admitting, "I had my first kiss this afternoon."

Almost in unison, her friends gasped. "Oh. My. *Gawd! Uuuuyyy! Ikaw na!* Who?"

"Blake Ryan," Krista mumbled. Warmth suffused her again.

"*Sino?*" Jenny couldn't hear.

"Her boss, the Hunk of Global City, Mr. Blake Ryan," Maddie told the others.

Blake received the moniker when he gained front cover exposure in a local magazine early this year. Maddie had come up with the title. Krista bought two copies like a teenaged fangirl. She had wrapped one in a protective plastic cover and the other she read, dog-earing the pages of his interview.

"He's so yummy!" Jenny gushed. At Lisa's reminder that she was a married woman, Jenny shot back, "True, but I'm not blind. I can look, right?" Slyly she added, "Krista can do the touching for me."

"So, how was it?" Lisa pressed.

Looking up at the ceiling, Krista leaned back in her chair and searched for the right words to describe such a life-altering event. "It was spicy ... but sweet ... hot and cold ... soft and tender, but also hard and firm. It seemed like it took hours, but it was mere seconds ..." Her gaze went back to meet her friends' quiet regard. "Unforgettable. It was a kiss to remember forever." She offered a weak smile, suddenly craving to be alone with her thoughts.

Angela cleared her throat. "Well, congratulations! It seems well worth the wait. Kudos for getting Superman to give you your first kiss." She looked at Krista searchingly as if gauging her mood then started excusing herself. "Gotta go, bitches! I have a flight to Bangkok tonight then Koh Samui after that." She blew Krista a kiss and admonished, "Don't do anything I wouldn't do, *m'amie*. Love you, babe. Advance happy birthday!"

"Thanks, Gie. That's a short list, though. Is there even anything you wouldn't do?" Krista teased. "Seriously guys, thank you for your birthday gift. You're so incredibly generous. This place is really private. It's peak season, and yet I haven't seen anyone but Blake and the staff. Not even the people who were on the same flight with me."

"You're welcome," Lisa replied. "Hey, I have to go, too. See you on November 8 for Sheila's memorial."

Jenny chimed in, "You deserve it, girlie. You've done without luxuries all your life. Enjoy yourself. Like our motto says—seize the day!" She added cheekily, "Oh, and seize the Blake."

After a chorus of "happy birthday," the three women signed off. Only Maddie remained online.

Of the five in the group, Krista considered Maddie her best friend. They had been roommates at the all-girls dormitory on the university campus. Both had the same zodiac sign—Scorpio—being born a week apart. Both had foreign fathers, Filipina mothers.

She had always thought of Maddie as her mirror image—the thinner, more confident version of herself. Krista arrived in college extremely overweight, with food her solace throughout her torturous high school years. Maddie, on the other hand, was almost emaciated. Her modeling career had pushed her into eating disorders to keep up with the competition for top jobs. Their mutual support in developing strong and healthy bodies reinforced the ties that bound their friendship.

Right now, however, her friend's pursed lips indicated something like worry. It made Krista uneasy. "Mads, tell me what you're thinking," she implored. "It isn't like you to be quiet. Aren't you happy for me?"

"Oh, Krissy," Maddie cried out, shaking her head vehemently. "Don't ever think that. I am incredibly happy for you. I've wanted you to break out of your shell for ages. I love that you've finally decided to focus on yourself instead of always putting others first."

"But …" Krista prompted. Maddie's words didn't match the skeptical expression on her face.

"But," Maddie exhaled. "I want you to be careful. I want you to protect your heart. Blake has the potential of being able to break it."

"Mads, it was just a kiss," Krista protested half-heartedly.

"Krissy, we both know it wasn't just a kiss," Maddie chided her. "Let's not pretend you're not already feeling so much more for Blake than you've ever felt for any guy who ever tried to court you." As usual, Maddie hit it right on the head.

"As if there were so many of those," Krista scoffed. "You can count on one hand the number of guys who as much as attempted to talk to me."

"Precisely my point!" Maddie bit out. "Because they don't matter. They haven't gotten through your protective walls. Blake breached them in such a short time. You only arrived there in Boracay this morning, and by the middle of the day he already kissed you. Whoa! That's fast, even for me."

"Madeleine! That's not fair. I've known him since May. It isn't as if we met today." She was getting steamed now. "Wasn't it you who arranged for me to be in this resort? Is Blake a part-owner here? If he is and you knew he was going to be here, why would you put me in his vicinity if you're so against him?"

Maddie had the grace to look a little shamefaced. "Yes, Blake is a partner there. He isn't advertising the fact, so don't tell anybody. When we had a meeting a couple of weeks ago, he told me in passing he was going to be in Boracay this coming week. It's truly a fabulous place, and I thought you could use the pampering, so I suggested it to the group. Plus, he gave me a good deal. That's why we chose Perlas." She paused for a moment. "I am not anti-Blake at all. As a matter of fact, I like him very much. I consider him a friend. You know me; I don't make male friends easily. They are either lovers or enemies."

"Well, then, you should explain your lack of enthusiasm about us, because I truly don't understand," Krista said testily. "Unless … you think I'm not good enough for him. Do you?"

"Don't be ridiculous!" Maddie exploded, then subsided just as fast. "You are the finest person I've ever known. It's Blake who's not nearly good enough for you. He's an experienced seducer, Krissy. A player. He eats little innocents like you for breakfast," she explained earnestly.

The heavy weight on Krista's heart lifted upon hearing the love and caring in her best friend's voice.

"He claimed he eats them for dinner, not lunch. He might also mean breakfast, huh?" she joked, happy to end their quarrel. She smiled in relief when Maddie let out a laugh. Taking a deep breath, she admitted, "Mads, what I didn't tell the others is that I've decided to give up my virginity. I've chosen Blake to help me with that."

Maddie nodded, seeming unsurprised with this revelation. "Yeah, I suspected. All your romance novel readings must have finally taken root." Leaning forward, she prodded some more. "Are you really, really sure you want to do this, *m'amie*? Once torn, your hymen won't grow back. I'm sorry for being crude, but are you certain you don't want to wait until you're married and give yourself to your husband?"

Krista let out a weary sigh. "When will that be, Mads? There are so many things happening in the world that scare me. Life is too short."

Wide-eyed, she continued to rationalize. "This morning when I had the brainstorm to adapt a new attitude in life, I thought to myself what if the plane crashed? What if I go out in a boat tomorrow and there's a typhoon, and I drown like Sheila did? There are a million things I haven't done yet. I don't want to have regrets when I die. I saw Blake here, and I felt the sparks we strike off each other. I've never felt this way with anyone. What guarantee is there that I'll have this kind of attraction with someone else ever again?"

Maddie was quick to offer encouragement. "I understand, sweetie. I do have the same fears as you. If you're sure, then you have my complete support. And if it makes you feel better, I think you made an excellent choice of a partner in this cherry-popping activity. Blake is quite sexy. And, he truly is interested in you. He's been grilling me about you ever since you joined his company." Maddie pouted, as if momentarily insulted that a man would prefer to talk about another woman in her presence.

"I have no personal knowledge of this since we only went out for drinks, but I've heard whispers about his excellent bedroom skills. Apparently, going to bed with him is a momentous occasion. Speaking of which, when will you be doing the bedroom tango?" She wiggled her eyebrows at her friend.

Krista burst out laughing. "Hey! I'm not so much of an obsessive-compulsive that I'd schedule sex on my calendar." While miming a writing action, she sing-songed, "Deflowering–Wednesday—November 2nd—nine pm." They both broke into giggles.

"Good luck on making him wait that long. Knowing his type, I'll bet he's planning to get you into his bed as early as tonight," Maddie declared. "I'm shocked you're not there already."

"He was such a gentleman earlier. He stopped after the kiss. I could tell it was hard—pun fully intended—for him to do that." Krista sniggered. "That's why I feel confident about my decision. I think he'll respect my feelings and go along with my choice of when I'm ready to take the next step," she said with certainty. The two friends grinned at each other at that declaration.

Suddenly remembering her suspicion about her friends' scheme, Krista blurted, "Is Blake part of the plan?" She had forgotten to ask earlier when everyone was online.

"What plan?" Maddie's confusion seemed genuine. Furrows appeared between her brows.

"You know. Boracay, Perlas, the form-fitting outfits, the makeover, the scheme to help me accomplish my Turning-Thirty Vow—*that* plan. Is Blake part of it?"

The guilty flush on Maddie's face said it all.

"What the hell were all your objections about him, then?" Krista yelled in exasperation. Her friend's name suited her perfectly. She was truly mad.

"We all wanted the real you to come out, and we were right. Look at you now. You're so sexy,"

Maddie said defensively. "The other three didn't know about Blake being there, but they hoped you'd meet someone within the week. I started having misgivings about including him in the scheme and playing Cupid, so I threw all those questions at you. But you blew all my doubts away. I want you to be sure of your decisions. I don't want you to have regrets later."

When she put it like that, their whole angst-filled conversation made sense. Krista shook her head at her meddling friend. "You are insane. You know that, right?"

"Maybe so, but you still love me anyway," Maddie laughingly agreed. "*Bonne chance, m'amie.* Again, guard your heart. This is simply physical, okay? Be careful you don't have your first heartbreak to go along with your first kiss and first lover. Don't fall in love with Blake. Your mom won't approve. Whatever happens, I'll be here for you always. *Je t'adore, mabiche.*" She sent off a few flying kisses and signed off.

Krista stayed in front of the computer for a long time. *No. There will be no regrets. There can't be. It will only be for one week, after all.*

Chapter Six

Jeepney [jip-nee] n. – a public utility vehicle. The most popular mode of transportation in the Philippines.

Blake knocked on the back door of Krista's cottage at exactly five thirty. He knew Filipinos were notorious for their tardiness, but he had never observed her exhibiting that poor behavior in all the time she'd worked for his company.

When she opened the door, he was again astonished at the dramatic difference that leaving her hair down and removing her glasses made to her appearance. She looked young, carefree, and tremendously alluring.

"Hello, beautiful," Blake greeted her warmly. Her response was a tepid smile.

She wore an empire-style short-sleeved floral dress with the hem above her knees. On her feet were a pair of red sandals with jeweled butterflies. He took note of her fondness for red footwear.

"I wish I had flowers to offer you, but I came empty-handed," he said regretfully. He bent to kiss her on the cheek and followed her into the cottage.

She appeared almost dainty when she wore flats. At the office she towered over her coworkers, especially when she wore high heels, which brought her to nearly six feet tall at times.

"Why do you have to bring me flowers? Is this a date?" She raised her eyebrow in inquiry.

She was challenging him, the saucy minx. He liked that. Most of the Filipino women he met pretended to be coy around him. "You tell me," he retorted. "You're the one who asked me to dinner this afternoon." He enjoyed teasing this woman. Her reactions were entertaining and refreshingly honest.

"I didn't ask you out to dinner. I merely inquired whether we were going to be at the same place at the same time," she said indignantly. "In any case, I already have enough flowers on my dress, so I'm good. Thank you very much."

He didn't think she was all that grateful. *Is she trying to keep me at arm's length again?*

"It's my bad then." He put his hands up in mock surrender, keeping his tone light. "It's just as well we're not on a date, as I'm not dressed for it," he gestured to his t-shirt, jeans, and flip flops, which were his weekend uniform, even in the city.

"I like it. You don't look like a CEO of a billion-dollar company."

"How is a CEO supposed to look like?"

"Old, fat, and bald," Krista sassily replied, grinning up at him.

He met her gaze with a knowing smile, amused by, and at the same time understanding of her hot and cold attitude this evening. It was another testament to her innocence that she wasn't an expert on the sexual games men and women play.

"The cart should be waiting outside to take us around. Shall we go?" At her nod, he moved towards the front door and opened it.

"Oh, this is nice!" she said when she saw the horse-driven modernized *karitela*—a four-seater, *nipa*-covered wagon—that sat outside. Her delight gratified him. Most of the guests were charmed by the tribute to the traditional vehicle. The locals were especially appreciative of the celebration of Filipino culture at Perlas.

Blake assisted Krista onto the first row of seats behind the driver, then pulled himself up to sit beside her. "So, what do you think of the *karitela*?"

"I think it's great. I haven't seen one used as a mode of transportation since I was a little girl." She smiled sweetly. "We used to visit my grandparents, my *lolo* and *lola* in Quezon. Back then, they still had those *carabao*-driven *karitons*, and *karitelas* like this one, taking the old folks around town. Now they are only brought out for ceremonial purposes during fiestas and *Santa Cruzan,* the May festival. I'm glad the resort has use for them."

"I was skeptical at first about having horses in the island, but the management won me over by taking care of them well. There is land where they can run, including the beach."

Blake produced a map from the vehicle's side pocket and pointed out the resort's vast acreage as the cart ambled along the path. Perlas was the only resort that offered beach rides on the stately animals, adding tremendously to what made them distinguishable from all the other resorts in Boracay.

On the map, the resort formed an irregularly shaped pentagon with three sides open to the water. The runway used by the private air-taxi marked the

length of the property on one side. On another side—
the one with the widest beachfront—the main
building was located. That was where most of the
guest activities were conducted.

Bluffs separated the main resort beach from
the semi-private beachfront area of the ten cottages.
Maharlika Kubo, the owners' cottage, was the biggest
and the last one on the right; the headland beside it,
which indicated the end of the property, was high and
steep.

It wasn't a long ride around the resort, even
though the property was expansive. The moment the
karitela stopped in front of the restaurant, Blake
dismounted and reached up to help Krista alight from
the cart.

Her sharp intake of breath at the touch of his
hands on her waist encouraged him to take his time,
deliberately brushing his body with hers the whole
way down. Her arms reflexively wrapped around his
neck to keep her balance during the descent.

He was tempted to kiss her when her cheeks
colored prettily; her eyes held a flare of desire before
she determinedly fixed her gaze on his throat.

It was hard to resist the lure of her full lips,
but he did it in part as a show of respect for her
modesty, and partly because he doubted his rein on
his self-control. He wasn't sure he could stop at mere
kissing, once he started.

***

Equal parts of relief and disappointment filled Krista when Blake released her with only a smile. She was sure he was going to kiss her again, but he moved back after she lowered her arms from around his neck.

He took her hand in his as they went into the restaurant and were shown their table by a uniformed waiter.

She was so confused. Her expertise at work and her ability to make sense of vast amounts of data and manipulate it into something her team could use were things she took pride in. But navigating relationship waters was beyond her. Now she regretted never having had a boyfriend.

Her heart-to-heart talk with Maddie influenced Krista to be more reserved around Blake. She still planned to sleep with him, but she needed to get to know him a whole lot more. It would not happen tonight; she was awfully tired.

She wished she could have had a nap this afternoon, but her talk with the girls had taken over an hour. There was barely enough time to shower before she had to meet Blake again.

At first, she thought he might be put off by her claim that tonight was not a date. His charming response coaxed her out of her reticence embarrassingly fast. *How can I guard my heart against him when there's so much there to like and admire?*

Blake could have taken credit for the karitela, but he acknowledged that it wasn't his idea and admitted initial skepticism about it. His recognition of the mistake spoke well of his integrity.

She knew from work that he earned the title of CEO through years of hard work and determination. It wasn't just handed to him because he was related to the owners, as was often done in the Philippines.

At lunch, she fibbed a little when she asked him how long he'd been in the country. She had researched him the moment she received access to the company's intranet.

His bio on the company website said he started as a junior marketing assistant and rose rapidly through the ranks. At twenty-eight years old he made vice-president in the head office, and when the former Philippine CEO retired, Blake was brought here to head the country office. From her study of the company's historical performance for the past fifty years, his management in the last five had taken the Philippine office to record levels of profitability.

His staff absolutely adored him, even though he was not demonstrative. To them he was beauty and brains personified. Their CEO was a fair boss, and she liked that he listened to his directors' opinions and advice, but he was firm with his decisions when he thought he was right.

In the office, Mr. Ryan was even-tempered. She'd never heard him raise his voice in anger. His quiet command was enough to silence arguments in the boardroom.

He could be cutting and abrupt at times, especially when the presentations went overly long and became frivolous, but he was never cruel.

She remembered the time the creative director of their advertising agency dramatically acted out the storyboard for their next commercial; Blake simply crossed his arms and cleared his throat. The flamboyant CD sobered up right away and got straight to the point.

Krista smiled at the memory, then nearly jumped in fright when somebody behind her cleared his throat and muttered in a clipped British accent, "Excuse me, Miss. I would really like to get some of those succulent prawns. Is it all right if I cut ahead of you?"

Her wool-gathering had taken her to the buffet tables, and she must have frozen in place. A short line had formed behind the tall, stunningly handsome man who looked exactly like the villain in the Thor and Avenger movies.

She flushed in embarrassment and stammered, "I, uhm, sorry. Please go ahead." She hastily grabbed a plateful of prawns when he was done, then nearly ran to the table where Blake waited for her. She dropped down on a chair beside him.

His lips twitched with suppressed laughter. He had witnessed the scene with the Hollywood actor and the prawns. Krista covered her face with her hands and groaned. *"Aargh!* That was so humiliating." Blake hooted with laughter; she reached over and hit him on the shoulder. "Stop laughing at me. It's not funny!"

"Ouch! You must not know your own strength, darling. That hurts." Blake grinned at her, rubbing his "injured" shoulder.

"Come on, now. You looked adorable matching the color of the seafood when you blushed. Also, you might have drooled a little when you saw him." He playfully wiped the side of her mouth with his thumb. She snarled at him and attempted to bite his offending finger, and he chuckled again.

"Cannibal," Blake teased. "So, what are your plans tomorrow?" He went back to eating. The three plates in front of him were piled high with assorted seafood.

He must work out a lot, she mused. *I know there's not an ounce of fat on that muscular body.* A frisson of heat rushed through her as she recalled the way her softness had melded with his hard form this afternoon.

Head bowed to hide her blush, she replied, "It's Sunday, so I'll probably go to mass in the morning. Then maybe I'll take a *jeepney* to D'Mall. My friends packed my luggage but left out a few things I need. I might grab some lunch there as well. What about you?"

"I wasn't planning to do anything but sleep, swim, and eat, which I usually do when I'm here. But you turned all my plans upside down ..." His tone turned serious. "And me inside out." He reached for her hand and threaded his fingers through hers. "Can I go with you?"

"To mass? I didn't know you're Catholic." He kept surprising her with revelations that matched her curiosity about him exactly. She left her hand in his, letting his thumb draw circles on her palm, making her tingle all over.

"Ah-huh. I'm Irish-Italian-American, what else would I be? I was even an altar boy when I was young, but lost my way when I learned about girls," he replied with a naughty grin. "I do go to church on Easter Sunday and Christmas Day, especially when I go back to New York to visit the folks. My mama insists, and I don't like disappointing my mother. She's not even five feet tall, but she can still kick my butt," he said with a fond look on his face.

"Aha! You're a mama's boy. I should have known you'd be spoiled," she said, only half-kidding. She removed her hand from his clasp. *Can this guy be for real? How could I not like a man who loves his mother and is not afraid to show it?*

"All of us three brothers are mama's boys," he conceded. "Just like my only sister is Daddy's girl."

This inside look into his life fascinated Krista. She didn't think anybody at the company knew this much about him. Maybe his secretary, Miss Malou, did; she must surely have received calls from his family when his cellphone was turned off, or when he left it on his desk during meetings.

This policy she agreed with—when they were in a meeting, he ordered that all mobile phones be left in lockers outside the conference room. This made the meetings go at a more efficient pace.

She had noticed Blake's absolute hatred of long meetings. Thirty minutes was his maximum limit. He'd cut in at the twenty-five-minute mark, tell the group to wind it down, and then he would leave. Many vendors and service providers had discovered how almost fanatical he was about this rule and adjusted their presentations accordingly.

Gah. Is there anything about this man I don't like or respect? If not for his arrogance, he'd be Mr. Perfect.

She nodded her head and replied jokingly, "If you're sure lightning won't strike when you enter the church, then yes, you can go with me." She stood up and declared, "I'm going to get dessert. Do you want anything?"

"I'm good, thanks. I don't like sweets at night." Patting his flat stomach, he added, "I'm so *busog*." He was so full. "Don't make Loki wait for the *leche flan* this time," he called, sniggering behind her back.

She turned around to poke her tongue out at him and pivoted towards the dessert table. *He is so annoying,* she thought with a smile. *There, he's not too perfect after all.*

SUNDAY

Chapter Seven

Bahala na [ba-ha-la-na] – "let fate take its course."
(A Filipino saying.)

As the priest droned on in his homily, Blake squirmed in his seat, frequently looking at his watch. *How could it still be just eight forty-five?* He gave himself a mental smack in the head for trying to impress Krista by going to church with her.

I am in a hell of my own making. First, he could not understand the Visayan language. Krista amazed him with her ability to follow the ceremony and say the right responses.

Second, he was sweating profusely because the church was stiflingly hot. It was packed with people, and the fan above his head wasn't working. In complete contrast to him, Krista looked cool in her cute little sundress and matching sandals, with her hair pulled back from her face in a loose ponytail. She even had a sarong wrapped around her shoulders; an improvised shawl for modesty.

Last, he was sleepy having stayed up late drinking Scotch whisky with the popular actor who was staying at the resort upon his invitation. The well-known thespian was the first choice to endorse their men's grooming line. He'd finally committed to it at two am. Blake came down to Boracay on Friday evening to speak with him, but the Hollywood star was ensconced in his cottage with the Do Not Disturb sign on the door.

Probably banging an island girl or two, Blake assumed uncharitably. He hoped it wasn't any of his staff, but even if it was, he couldn't act as the moral police to forbid them from doing something they wanted. As long as it was consensual and no money was exchanged; the partners wouldn't like having charges of prostitution directed against Perlas.

A poke on his side startled Blake. Krista was frowning down at him. The sermon had finally ended, and the congregation had risen for the recitation of the Nicene Creed.

Sheepishly, he got to his feet and started to pay attention. He recited the prayers in English, knelt and stood up at the proper times, and shook hands with his neighbors as a sign of peace. He gave Krista a peck on the cheek and held her hand during the singing of The Lord's Prayer, but did not go with her to take communion.

Blake was sixteen the last time he went to confession, for that sin of fornication. He didn't feel comfortable taking the body of Christ into his own without the benefit of absolution. If he decided to come clean about the sinful things he wanted to do with Krista, he would be in the confessional for hours.

Relief coursed through him when the priest gave the final blessing. He hastily made the sign of the cross and left the church before he overheated. Perlas kept an air-conditioned van in the main part of the island for the guests to use, and he needed the comfort of its cool interior. Not to mention the contents of the water cooler the resort kept fully stocked inside it.

Blake put on his sunglasses and waited impatiently for Krista to join him outside. She had told him earlier that she wanted to light a candle at the altar, so he left her to do it by herself.

Yes, he was being a dick, but his pounding head was a legitimate excuse for it. His body craved caffeine and something substantial to fill it ASAP. The bottled water he drank in practically one gulp helped, but he needed a good-sized steak right now. His head, too, could use a couple of ibuprofen. He'd have to blame being *hangry* and offer his apologies for his rude behavior.

To his relief, Krista didn't linger at the church. She got to the van faster than he expected. When everyone from the resort was accounted for, Blake signaled the driver to take them to D'Mall at Station 2, widely considered the island's central hub with its vast array of restaurants, cafes, boutiques, and shops.

"Do you mind if we eat first before shopping?" he asked Krista when they disembarked. "I didn't get any breakfast before we left for church— not even coffee. I'm starving."

He should have asked her during the short ride, but she wasn't talking to him. He kept quiet as well, since he didn't want the other passengers to overhear their conversation.

"I don't mind. I haven't eaten yet, either. Where do you want to go?"

He expected her to tell him off, but she acted gracious and understanding. His guilt increased; he needed to make amends. He'd buy her a gift, he decided as he watched her remove the makeshift shawl. She looked sexy in her spaghetti-strap dress. Maybe he'd get her something to match her outfit.

"I'm salivating for a big juicy steak and a plateful of garlic fried rice with eggs on top. Is the barbecue place fine with you?" The moment he mentioned food, his stomach rumbled. He groaned in embarrassment.

She let out a startled laugh. "Whoa! Clearly, your tummy doesn't care to hear my opinion. Let's go feed it."

***

Krista was glad to see Blake restored to his usual charming self after getting fed. He looked rough this morning. When she saw him approach from a distance, he looked bad-boy sexy with stubble on his jaw and sunglasses covering his eyes, which she would find out later were bloodshot. All he needed was a motorcycle and a leather jacket to complete the James Dean vibe he projected.

Scrap the leather jacket, she reconsidered. He had roasted in his black t-shirt and jeans at the crowded place of worship. He was restless in his seat nearly the whole duration of the mass. She could understand—even sympathize, knowing him now for six months—especially with his attitude towards long meetings.

The mass, conducted in the local language *Hiligaynon,* had lasted almost one and a half hours. Between the priest's lengthy and dragging homily and what seemed like the whole congregation taking communion, for a non-devout Catholic like Blake it must have been torture. No wonder he didn't go to services regularly.

No one could call Krista devout either, as she often missed mass to write papers for her master's degree or work overtime to earn extra pay. She went today because of her upcoming birthday, and because she wanted to give thanks for all the blessings she received this past year.

She nixed her initial plan to confess her future sin of engaging in pre-marital sex, since not being truly repentant would compound the transgression. Instead, she just said her prayers during the Penitential Act.

It might not even happen. She could still back out of sleeping with Blake at the last minute. If it did happen, she would examine her conscience afterwards and take it from there.

During lunch, Blake had kept apologizing to her.

"For what?" she'd asked.

"For my inattention at the mass and impatience to get out of the church. I'm hung-over from drinking with your British movie star."

"Ha! Serves you right." She smiled, thrilled at their inside joke.

"Ouch. Heartless wench." He smiled back. "I only slept a couple of hours. My older brother Aidan woke me up at the crack of dawn with a demanding phone call."

"Poor you." She laughed when he jutted out his lower lip in a mock-pout. "I'm kidding. There's nothing to forgive. I understand." It pleased her to witness another speck of imperfection in him.

Blake impressed her with his commitment to sit through the mass in abject discomfort because of her. He could have left at any time, especially during the homily, to sit in the air-conditioned van. But he stayed and suffered the boredom, heat, and the parishioners' stares.

Of the few foreigners inside the church, or outside for that matter, most were female and many of those were elderly. The tall, handsome, badass-looking hunk who sat beside her was one of a kind.

She prayed for the Lord's forgiveness for her vanity inside His house. Krista had felt a burst of pride when she saw women look at her with envy because she was with him. She sympathized with the awestruck teenage girl who stood in the pew in front of them, eyes wide and mouth open, as Blake shook her hand and said, "Peace be with you."

On the flip side, she was apprehensive that someone from the office might be in Boracay and see them together. *Bahala na,* Krista thought. *We haven't done anything wrong. Whatever will be, will be.*

Now, strolling through the shops, Krista excused herself to look at a pair of sandals that caught her eye. Blake nodded in agreement and said he wanted to check something out himself.

Shoes were her secret vice; the only fashion item her friends considered her the expert on. Now that she could afford them, Krista bought two pairs to add to her ever-growing collection. As she changed into one of her new pairs of sandals, she felt something touch her head. Blake had returned with a hat for her. Wide-brimmed, plain white, and made of straw, it would go well with anything she wore.

"I noticed you don't have one." He shrugged when she looked at him quizzically. "You have fair skin; you've got to protect it. You're getting sun-kissed right here." He tenderly tapped a finger on her cheekbone.

"Thanks, how thoughtful of you." Krista beamed a grateful smile, delighted that he was making up for his earlier grouchiness. She had planned to buy a couple of hats, so getting one as a present was something she truly appreciated.

"You are most welcome," he returned. "Here, I got you three." He revealed two similarly-styled black and red hats that he'd hidden behind his broad back and handed them to her.

She squealed and reached up to give him a lip-smacking kiss on the cheek, her delight for the gifts overcoming her reticence to show affection in public. "Thank you, thank you, and thank you! I love them." She faced the mirror and tried each one on. "Look! They match my outfit and shoes."

"They do. You would fit right in at the Kentucky Derby, looking like that."

"Or the Ascot races like Eliza Doolittle in *My Fair Lady*," she retorted, certain he wouldn't be familiar with the movie.

"The *rine* in *Spine sties minely* in the *pline*," he intoned, reciting the famous line in a pretend Cockney accent. He laughed at the surprise on her face. "Audrey Hepburn is my mom's favorite actress. She would watch *Breakfast at Tiffany's, Roman Holiday,* and *Sabrina,* etcetera, repeatedly." He bent down to help with her purchases and his presents, unaware of how charming she found his statement.

There he goes being amazing again. How can I resist such a well-rounded guy? She gave him a smile as he opened the boutique's doors for her. "Where to next?" he inquired.

"Can we go in there?" Krista pointed to a tattoo parlor. "I want to check out their designs." Both Maddie and Angela had a couple of tattoos, and she loved the idea of getting one herself.

She looked at Blake who was gaping at her in shock. "What? Don't you dare say you don't think I'm the type to get a tattoo, or I'll hit you." Yesterday, when he turned around to take his shower, she caught a glimpse of a large one on his back. She hadn't viewed it up close, but it looked to her like a family crest.

"Not gonna say anything." He closed his mouth and made a zipping motion with his thumb and forefinger. Then he opened the door to the studio and immediately broke his promise by saying, "After you, milady."

***

Whew! Blake was relieved when they left the tattoo studio fifteen minutes after they went in. Krista consulted with an artist and was advised against getting it done today. Part of post-tattoo care was to avoid swimming or soaking the new ink in water for up to four weeks.

Also, fresh tattoos needed at least ten to fourteen days of healing time before exposure to the sun. Since this was only her second day in the island, getting a tattoo now would severely limit her activities for the rest of the week. Krista pouted, but conceded the wisdom of it and instead made an appointment for Friday afternoon.

She might have shaken her fists at him, but she truly didn't seem the type to get inked. Call him a hypocrite—he had a large image of his Irish ancestors' coat of arms almost covering his whole back—but he'd never found tattoos attractive on a girl. Krista could change his mind.

From her gestures to the artist, it looked like she wanted the tattoo on her upper back or shoulder area. He looked closer as the artist sketched Krista's design and saw that she wanted the popular Latin maxim *"carpe diem"*.

From what he understood, those who took on *carpe diem* as their motto believed in making the most out of life in the present while they still could— of doing new things while they had the opportunity. He vaguely remembered the line from the movie *Dead Poets' Society*, where Robin Williams's character, Professor John Keating, told his students to seize the day and make their lives extraordinary. Or something like that.

This new resolve might have something to do with her upcoming birthday on Wednesday. It'd be her thirtieth, a milestone for a lot of people. Maddie mentioned it before, and again yesterday when she called him before he picked up Krista for dinner.

He shook his head and grimaced at the remembered conversation with the half-French spitfire. "Blake, I'm going to Perlas on Wednesday," she informed him haughtily. "It's going to be a surprise. Promise not to tell Krista."

She expected to stay at her friend's cottage on the second. As if he were her personal concierge, she wanted him to let the front desk know that she only needed the flight. After all, Krista's stay was charged on Maddie's credit card. *The woman has some gall.* He also suspected she planned to cockblock him. *Ha! Good luck with that.*

To complicate matters, his brother United States Air Force Lieutenant Colonel Aidan Garrick Ryan, Air Attaché at the US Embassy in Singapore, also came into the picture. He, too, wanted to come to Boracay on Wednesday, commanding that he only needed the flight, as he intended to bunk in with his little brother.

Blake was of a mind to get those two together. Yes. He would get Krista into his bed on Tuesday, then he'd stick Maddie and Aidan in her cottage on Wednesday. They could brawl like cats and dogs there, for all he cared. Blake chuckled and turned his thoughts back to Krista, who was browsing through some books at a second-hand shop.

So, that was what she was doing yesterday— seizing the day. He fondly recalled the previous day's transformation from the prim but spirited Ms. Lopez in the morning, to the *vavavoom* Krista just a couple of hours later. The one who responded to his kiss with a sensuality that enflamed him.

He wondered what other things she planned to seize. Whatever they were, he'd make sure his body was on the list.

He smiled at her when she came out of the bookshop. "All done? Want some ice cream?" He badly needed to cool down.

"Yes, please. A humongous banana split. With lots and lots of whipped cream and cherries." She clapped excitedly. *Oh yeah, this woman is darned sweet. I can't wait to taste her again.*

Chapter Eight

Duyan [doo-yan] n. – hammock.

Hmm, this is the life, Krista thought. Blake had called ahead to have the staff set up two portable bamboo hammocks outside his cottage. She put her book down and sighed in contentment as she relaxed on one of them, appreciating the cool afternoon breeze.

While Blake chose to swim, to burn off the calories from their ice cream dessert, Krista preferred to lounge around by the beach. She supposed she could have done some yoga, but the lure of just chilling out was too tempting to resist. *Who's being lazy now?* she mocked herself.

When she came out of her *kubo* wearing a yellow bikini, Krista saw a couple of their neighbors also out on the sand. She was reassured by the distance between them, enough to not feel self-conscious about her near-nakedness. Though still unused to wearing so little, feeling free and unrestricted was quickly growing on her.

She reached back to fluff the pillow under her head and burrowed deeper into it, realizing that getting a tattoo today would have been an extremely bad idea. Not that she was the best swimmer, but being unable to get into the sea or the whirlpool in her cottage's garden would totally suck. This way, she could still go scuba diving, jet skiing, and parasailing. Blake helped arrange all those plans for the next couple of days.

Krista turned onto her front. She didn't see anybody paying attention to her, and the sides of the hammock hid her from view, so she untied the bikini strings on her back. If she was going to tan, it might as well be even. The sun, mildly warm this time in the late afternoon, made her glad.

Touching the area where *"Carpe Diem"* would be inked on Friday, she thought again of the consequences of getting it done too early—pain for the rest of the night and then a scabby, itchy back for the rest of the week as the tattoo healed.

Yikes! That would certainly not be terribly attractive to Blake. Terrible maybe, but attractive? A big no.

Although, she supposed, *he will absolutely love putting the ointment on my back. He will take his time tracing every letter of the words and every curve of the vines with his fingers. His stroke will be gentle, but his touch will be oh, so, hot.* The imagined caress made her tremble.

She gasped in shock at the cool fingers tracing the line where the strings once met at the middle of her back. *Why is his touch so familiar already, when I've only known its feel for one day?*

"Blake," she sighed as she bit back a moan. His fingers continued to draw circles over her shoulders, occasionally flicking stray hairs that escaped her topknot. The hammock dipped as he added his weight to hers; the support creaked but held firm.

"Is this where you're going to put it?" He spelled the letters C-A-R-P-E-D-I-E-M exactly where she told the tattoo artist she wanted them. His damp skin and wet swim shorts touched her entire left side, but the sensation was not uncomfortable. It felt refreshing, her body now heated by his caresses.

"Y-y-yes," she breathed out. Her back arched to follow his touch when he started to pull his fingers away. She kept her head buried on the pillow, sure that her face would show the intensity of her desire.

"*Sssh.*" His hot breath stirred the hairs at the back of her neck. He hadn't moved away at all. He'd shifted closer, to replace his fingers with his lips. She started to turn over, but he gently but firmly held her shoulder to keep her where she was. "Not yet," he whispered, "I'm only at the D."

He took his sweet time torturing her. She wanted his mouth on hers right now. Just as she thought she was ready to scream, his hands on her hips flipped her over. The sudden movement caused the hammock to shake. He pulled her left leg over his hip, opening her up; his hard knee nudged her most sensitive flesh.

Her breath caught in her throat when the cool air touched her bare breasts. She raised her arms to cover them, but Blake was quicker. He captured both her hands in his, leaving her exposed. Her head whipped to the side to see if there were still people around. To her relief, she saw no one.

The sun had dipped to the horizon on the other side of the island, but Perlas' side was still sunlit, the sky painted with splashes of purple and orange shades.

She looked at Blake in mute appeal, heat suffusing her face and body at the thought of being made love to in the open, but he simply brushed her knuckles with his lips. "You're gorgeous, Krista. Don't hide yourself from me."

Only when she nodded did he release her hands, placing them to the sides of her body. She held herself stiffly at first, but the heat in his gaze as they roamed over her, gradually loosened her rigid muscles. His nostrils flared when she moistened her suddenly dry lips with her tongue.

Bending as if to kiss her, Blake traced the shape of her mouth with his thumb instead. He was surely a secret sadist; this slow torment was just plain cruel. She wanted to get back at him for the agony he was causing her by taking his finger into her mouth, but he evaded her seeking lips and shook his head.

He ran his fingers down her neck, traced her collarbone on both sides, then dipped his thumb lightly into the hollow of her throat.

Her breath caught when the pad of his palm pressed on the round flesh of her right breast. He paused on the inner curve of her breast as if measuring her heartbeat. His left hand mirrored the actions of his right, both hands now circling her round flesh, drawing closer and closer to her nipples but never quite getting there.

"Tell me what you desire, baby," Blake urged gently, his voice rough. "What do you want me to do?"

Krista's nipples ached for his touch. Between her legs, she felt a trickle of dampness flow, making her bikini bottom wet. "Touch me … kiss me …" she moaned, offering her body to him.

Her hand gripped his right shoulder, her fingernails dug into his muscles, leaving half-moon marks. She cried out when Blake's fingers finally enclosed her nipple and pulled gently. Her head thrashed on the pillow when he bent to lick the hardened nub and close his teeth around the tip. Her back bowed as his hands pulled her closer, and his mouth opened wider to take more of her flesh in. She wrapped her arms around his neck and rolled her hips as he moved to lavish the same treatment on her left breast.

The hammock swayed when Blake removed his knee from between her legs to replace it with the hardness of his full arousal. Only two damp pieces of clothing kept them from a complete joining.

Something was building inside her, but she didn't know how to get relief from it. "Blake … please …" she begged. For what, she didn't know. What she knew was that only he could give it to her.

He moved his hands to her bottom and locked their lower bodies together, his rock-hard cock rubbing faster against her flimsily covered mound.

Her mind emptied of thought, her body filled with sensations—heat, friction, speed, light. The pleasure ratcheted up and finally burst as he tore his lips away from her breast and fastened them onto her mouth, swallowing her scream of release.

***

Blake gathered Krista close, feeling the early dusk air cool down their heated bodies. He searched beneath him for the sarong she discarded earlier and pulled it over them to keep away most of the breeze coming from the sea. He rubbed down the goosebumps that started to break out on her skin. *Her first orgasm,* he realized. What gifts she had bestowed on him with her first kiss yesterday and now her first orgasm.

When he came out of the water and saw her lying nearly naked on the hammock, he almost fell to his knees as the desire for her slammed into him.

His gaze roamed over her smooth skin, and he questioned her desire to blemish it permanently with black ink. But, it was her body, her choice. He had no option but to accept her decision as long as she was happy with it.

He understood now how important it was to her to live up to the principles of the motto she'd recently embraced. Krista had told him about her friends from college—about Sheila who inspired the dictum, and her belated commitment to fulfill the promise they all made to their deceased friend. The vow was to seize every moment that came their way, and make the most of their time in the present. That was why she wanted to try doing things she had never done. He had promised to assist her in making all of them happen.

Every second they spent together revealed more and more about Krista. What he knew so far impressed him greatly. His attraction to her evolved in a totally unusual way than his norm with every other woman he'd dated. He noticed her for her brain before he came to appreciate her physical beauty. After what they had just done, there was no question about her desirability now or ever.

Their lovemaking went further than Blake expected. He had only planned to touch her, but her passionate response was his undoing.

When he gazed upon the bounty of her breasts bared for the first time, he offered up a prayer of gratitude to the Creator for making such a perfect being. And when he tasted her, how sweet and soft she was. But hard, too. His mouth watered at the idea of taking her taut nipples into his mouth again. His hands tightened on her back as he fought the urge to feel the weight of her luscious breasts once more.

He'd tried to take his time; he truly did. But her throaty moans and husky entreaties egged him on until he was out of his mind with the need to come. Somehow, he found the strength to remain in control of his body and hold off his climax.

When he finally let himself come, it would be inside her. *What an explosion it will be.* Just then, color burst from the sky to his left, perfectly matching the image that popped into his head.

Krista's head lifted at the noise. "What's that?" She felt around for her bikini top and to his disappointment, put it back on.

"Fireworks," he said, sitting up and pulling her body to rest on his chest. He arranged the sarong to cover her front, then wrapped his arms around her. "Perlas puts on a display every Sunday to signal the end of the week and welcome a new one."

"Nice, but why not Friday? Isn't that when most guests arrive?" She nestled closer, seeking his warmth. The sun had fully set, and the night air had cooled considerably. Faint illumination was provided by the fireworks and the *tiki* torches that guarded the entrance to each cottage.

"They can do Fridays too," he promised her. *If she wants fireworks on Friday, I'll make sure there is a display this coming weekend.*

"Hey, are you hungry, sweetie?" He liked having her close, but he was starting to itch from the sand and salt, and his swim shorts needed to be thrown in the wash.

She yawned. "Yeah, but I want something light, like soup or salad. I'd like to sleep early, too. We got a lot planned for tomorrow." She moved to get off the hammock, so he gave her a little push to aid her ascent. He heard her murmur of thanks as she looked around for her stuff.

Seeing Krista yawn made Blake realize that he was beat. He'd been operating on only four hours of sleep, and he hadn't fully shaken off the effects of the alcohol yet.

Dismounting from the hammock, he took her hand to walk her back to her cottage. He halted at the beginning of the path that marked the entrance to her *kubo*. Their day together was at an end. He had to hit the pause button on his seduction plan right here.

"Thanks for letting me spend the day with you. I had fun." He didn't lie. He'd truly enjoyed being with her, especially during the past hour. He could spend the next five days doing what they did in that hour, over and over again.

"I did, too." She reached out a hand to touch his jaw, her soft palm brushing against his bristly stubbles. She raised herself on tiptoes to plant a gentle kiss on his lips. "Goodnight, Blake."

He caught the back of her neck lest she move away. That measly peck didn't satisfy him. *What am I, five years old?*

He pressed her closer, slanted his mouth over hers, and gave her an adult kiss—a kiss that mimicked the sexual act they hadn't yet engaged in but soon would. His lips worked hers open, his tongue tangled with hers before he let her go.

Blake stepped back, looking with satisfaction at Krista's flushed cheeks and the plumpness of her just-kissed lips. *Now,* that *was a proper goodnight kiss.* "Goodnight, Krista. Sweet dreams."

MONDAY

Chapter Nine

Tatay [ta-tie] n. – father.

It is indeed better and wetter under the sea. Krista kept thinking of the tune from *The Little Mermaid* as she, Blake, and Dencio, the Perlas' Dive Master, hovered near Friday's Rock, a fish-feeding station that was probably the most popular scuba diving site in Boracay. Because its bottom was only eighteen meters deep, all levels of divers could go there.

It didn't surprise her that Blake was certified as an Advanced Scuba Diver. More astonishing would be to discover the things he couldn't do rather than those he could. The man was just so darned impressive.

Look at him now with his fancy underwater camera, taking close-up photos of the colorful fishes. She would love to see the pictures later; now, she wanted to take in the astounding marvel of this underwater world. She smiled widely, nearly dislodging her regulator from her mouth, when a school of striped fish passed by and she thought she saw Nemo. *All I know of marine life, I learned from cartoon movies.*

She blinked when she saw Blake. He'd swum closer to take pictures of her. Scowling, she covered her face with her gloved hands. *Ugh.* How anyone could look good wearing a full-face diving mask was beyond her. They tussled playfully underwater. Blake swam around trying to capture her expressions while she kept turning away.

Their fun was interrupted by Dencio, the spoilsport DM, who signaled thumbs up, meaning they should ascend. It was the end of the dive. That hand signal was one of the first things she learned this morning when she sat down for the crash course in scuba diving.

Being with Blake and a Dive Master allowed Krista to go in open water. However, if she wanted to dive in the future, she would need a certificate. She thought she would do exactly that; it had been so much fun.

On the boat for their return trip to the resort, she said as much to Blake. She gave an okay sign— thumb and index finger forming a loop, the other three fingers extended—to both the dive and to removing the heavy equipment from her body. She couldn't wait to get back to land and take off the neoprene suit as well, but that was a minor complaint compared to the wondrous experience she just had.

Comfortably dressed now in one of the tank tops and shorts ensembles from her island wardrobe, Krista perused the lunch menu at one of Perlas' restaurants and made a face.

"What's the matter?" asked Blake. He had also showered and changed into a t-shirt and shorts.

Looking at him, she wondered why the company had hired the Hollywood actor to endorse their male grooming line. Blake could do an excellent job himself. Even better, they would save money on talent fees.

In marked contrast to yesterday's five o'clock shadow, Blake's face was clean shaven. She blushed remembering how the bristles on his jaw left chafe marks on her breasts.

She shook her head at the dangerous direction her thoughts were taking. "I don't think I can eat fish ever again after seeing those colorful creatures today." She grinned at Blake. "Did you take a picture of Nemo?"

Blake laughed. "No, but I found Dory."

This guy gets me. He really does. The waiter interrupted their amusement to take their orders— chicken *inasal* for Blake, and La Paz *batchoy* for Krista. Both dishes hailed from Western Visayas, the same region as Boracay.

"I can see now why my friend Angela loves scuba diving. That was incredible! I'm sure she's having so much fun in Koh Samui right now," she told Blake. Angela also had advanced certification.

"Koh Samui? Does she live there? My brother Craig is there, too. He's the executive chef at one of the major hotels in the island." She heard Blake's pride in his brother's accomplishment in his voice. His closeness to his family was another thing they had in common.

"No, Angela owns a travel adventure company. She's on the island for a couple of weeks to network and to see how her Thai counterparts do things, so she can replicate them in the Philippines," she explained. "I'll text her to check out your brother's restaurant while she's there. She loves good food as much as I do. She's this tiny little thing, a little over five feet tall, but boy, can she eat."

Then she remembered something he said earlier. "Wait, your other brother is Aidan, you're Blake, and now there's Craig. A-B-C. Let me guess, your sister's name begins with a D!" She chortled when Blake groaned, amused by how that naming convention was so like the Filipinos'.

"Darcy—the runt of the family is named Darcy," he confirmed. He brought out his phone and clicked on the photos app.

She gasped when she saw a studio portrait of the Ryans. "You have a gorgeous family, Blake." Not surprising, really. But she was blinded by all that beauty in one photo.

"Thanks. That was taken last year after Aidan's promotion to lieutenant colonel." Blake pointed to the commanding figure of a military officer in dress uniform who could pass for his twin, only leaner and more stern-looking. He handed the phone to Krista so she could take a closer look.

Aidan, Blake, and Darcy all looked like their mother, who was still pretty for a woman Krista guessed to be in her late fifties. Craig, on the other hand, was a carbon copy of their dad. Both built like bruisers, but they had warm smiles.

It was easy to see why Blake called Darcy the runt. Not only was she much younger than her brothers—probably mid-twenties compared to their thirties age range—but also of medium height and slender build. The only girl had the black hair and blue eyes that ran in the family's DNA, and they looked stunning on her. The Ryan family was most certainly a supremely photogenic clan.

Krista handed the phone back to him, suddenly missing her parents and siblings. This was her first birthday without them. She'd just have to try to get them on a video call on Wednesday. Her father hated the impersonality of modern technology, but as a former teacher, he respected the genius of their inventors.

"Food. Yes." Blake cheered when he saw the waiter approach with their order. "*Gutom na ako. Sobra,*" he said in Filipino, meaning he was ravenous. She couldn't help but be charmed by his occasional lapses into her native language.

"How did you learn Filipino? Did you take classes?" She dug into her *batchoy*—a soup made with pork organs, crushed pork cracklings, chicken stock, beef loin, and round noodles that originated in the district of La Paz, Iloilo City.

"From my aunt," Blake replied.

"You're part-*Pinoy*?" Her jaw dropped at his statement.

"Unfortunately, no. I have an honorary aunt who is Filipina. We call her Tita Belen. She's the cook at the pub my father co-owns in Hell's Kitchen. Her husband, Uncle Jack—also Irish-American—is my dad's business partner. They're my parents' best friends, and their two sons, Patrick and Ronan, grew up with us."

"She must have been happy that you're working in the Philippines, her native land," Krista commented, but she barely listened to Blake's response. She applied herself to her food and only nodded absently when he excused himself to take a phone call.

A Filipina and Irish-American pairing that worked? That puts ideas in my head, doesn't it? Dare I hope that something more can develop from the physical attraction between us? Can there be something to look forward to beyond this week?

The American and Filipina unions that she knew of didn't make it—they'd all divorced, with the women coming back to the Philippines much worse off than when they left.

Would her own parents have done well together? If her biological father had known her mom was pregnant, would he have come back to marry her? She loved her *tatay,* the man who raised her as his own, but something in her called out to finding her real father. Krista acknowledged the futility of such thoughts, but she couldn't help the longing inside.

"*Aray!*" The simultaneous exclamation of pain, the heavy thud of a body hitting the floor, and the crash of glass snapped her out of her reverie and onto the tableau in front of her.

Blake bent to help a server to her feet, offering his apologies for bumping into her. He got down on his knees, assisting in the clean-up, putting the nervous girl at ease. He took Krista's breath away. He should have looked subservient in that position—humble, diminished. But, no. His kindness enhanced his masculinity and his strength.

Oh, Krista. If you're not careful, that girl won't be the only one who fell because of Blake. You will, too. Harder. With no chance of being able to get up. *The question is, would I really want to?*

"No …Yes … I don't know."

"You don't know what?" Blake was back on his seat beside her.

"Uhm, I don't know how you keep any employees if you mow them down like that," she said teasingly. *Good save, Krista.*

Blake laughed. "Yeah, I'm such a klutz. We have to double their salaries and workers' compensation insurance to get them to stay with Perlas." His appreciative gaze roamed over her face, showing his liking for her humor. He reached for her hand. "Sweetheart, I know I promised to spend the day with you, but I'm going to have to beg off this afternoon. Some urgent business came up with the resort and since I'm the only partner in residence, I have to take charge."

She squeezed his hand in reassurance. "That's okay. I'm a big girl. I'm sure I can find things to do. If not, I can always read and just relax. Don't worry about me. I'll be fine."

"Thanks. Dinner later?" At her nod, he gave her a quick peck on the cheek and left. She watched as his long strides took him away from her.

That, Krista, is why you should be able to get up if you fall. She must get used to seeing his back as he left her. Because he would. Eventually.

***

Krista selected the cabana as the best place to relax. The sun was very hot, so she chose not to go for a walk on the beach. Instead, she did the yoga exercises she had been neglecting since arriving on the island. She didn't want to stay inside her *kubo* after her workout; it wasn't much different from being in her condo in Makati. She also had no desire to get wet again after being in the water all morning, but she liked the view her small garden pool offered.

A massage so soon after lunch didn't appeal to her, so she booked a session for another day. All the unaccustomed exercise from this morning, and that she planned to subject her body to in the coming days, would surely leave her aching. If she went ahead with her plan to go to bed with Blake on Wednesday night, she'd need the spa even more on Thursday. Krista sighed. "Who am I kidding? Sleeping with Blake is not a question of if, but when."

Krista posted a few pictures of the dive on her online diary page, then grabbed her romance novel and eyeglasses. Adding to her pile a bottle of cold water, one of the hats that Blake gave her, and a towel, she headed to the cabana and its sunbeds. With the fan overhead stirring the air made fragrant by the ylang-ylang flowers in the garden, Krista should have been as comfortable as anyone could be. *Except that I am not comfy—far from it, in fact.*

The love scene in the book was not helping lower her body's temperature. The author's description of the couple's lovemaking was far too reminiscent of last night's make-out session. Only she and Blake didn't go all the way like the fictional

90

lovers in the book, who consummated their relationship on the night they met.

Could I have slept with Blake right after my job interview last April? Krista flushed at the thought. *No, even knowing how great he is, it wouldn't have happened.* Neither of them were hit by insta-lust that day, as far as she could tell.

Yes, she found him handsome—but cold. And she was certain he didn't salivate at the thought of taking such a buttoned-up schoolmarm to bed at that time. Krista laughed out loud at the ludicrous image of Mr. Ryan and Ms. Lopez, both wearing pinstriped suits, getting it on in the boardroom. Not even her favorite author could write that scene and make it sexy.

She shook her head and looked around. *No, it's this place. It's Boracay.* No one could possibly be immune to its allure. The cerulean sky, the pristine white sand, the calm turquoise waters, and the clean, breathable air provided a perfect backdrop for romance to breed and grow.

The two of them had needed these past six months to get to know one another. She needed him to see her as his intellectual equal before he saw her as a passionate female. Her friends had to force her to come to Boracay and leave her virtually naked before she could liberate herself of self-imposed restrictions and go after her repressed wants.

The book on her lap caught her attention again. This and others like it had been her solace during these years of romantic barrenness. They might have also caused impossible expectations in her when it came to finding love. The novels always described an undefinable chemistry that existed between two people who were supposed to be right for each other—always an electricity when they touched. She thought it was only fiction, until Blake.

Her outburst on Saturday morning proved how the feelings he evoked in her were different to those of every other man she had met. Chemistry, electricity, sparks, and fireworks. They were all there when they touched … when they kissed.

Krista hugged the book to her chest. This was where she got the idea of losing her virginity on her thirtieth birthday this week. This was why she was still chaste but not altogether ignorant of the sexual act.

In her favorite old-school romances, especially the historical novels, a woman was considered on the shelf—an old maid—by her late twenties. Although the twenty-first century had arrived, and the stigma was no longer visited upon those who chose single-blessedness, Krista surely didn't want to be one of them.

She wanted to fall in love, get married, and have children someday. But if that day never came, she wanted to be able to say that she at least had experienced being made love to by someone she had positive feelings for.

That made Blake the perfect person for the job. Not only because he was right here, right now, but also because he was the right man.

Positive feelings were words too tame to describe what she already felt for Blake. Attraction, infatuation, and passion were far more apt. He had said he wanted her—lusted after her. It wasn't love, but for the meantime it was enough. At least for this week, until Friday night, Krista knew he was all hers.

That's what my mindset should be. Just think of this week. Take each day as it comes: isn't that the essence of carpe diem*? Don't think of Saturday, when it's time to go back to Makati. Don't think we'll become Tita Belen and Uncle Jack 2.0. Don't think of Happily Ever After, for therein lies heartbreak. That's for fairy tales, not for real life.*

She had already promised her virginity to Blake, and she would not renege on it, Catholic guilt notwithstanding. If last night was any indication, she wouldn't regret making that choice. She had her first orgasm, even without penetration. *It only happens in books.*

Krista looked down at her book again and smiled as an idea began to form in her head. So far, he had been in command of their lovemaking. Maybe next time she would take the initiative.

"Wouldn't that surprise Mr. Blake I-Will-Teach-You-All-You-Need-To-Know Ryan?"

Chapter Ten

Ulan [oo-lan] n. – rain.

Blake was annoyed by the length of time it took to wrap up the business concerns that cut his afternoon off with Krista. Because they were all in different time zones, it took four hours to get all the partners together on video conference to agree to a decision and finalize their response.

Then there was this stupid rain, which was not in any weather forecast. Rains were not totally unexpected; they were on a tropical island, after all. A little warning would have been great, though. Blake hoped it wouldn't rain again the following night, because he had a plan for Krista's birthday dinner that would take them outdoors.

He wanted to celebrate Krista's Turning-Thirty party for the next two nights. Tuesday was for just the two of them; Madeleine and Aidan were set to show up on Wednesday morning. There'd be another celebration that evening.

He jogged to Krista's cottage using the front entrance instead of the path from the beach. He didn't want to track wet sand all over her *kubo*. She greeted him with a dazzling smile that wiped his afternoon frustrations away. She looked so pretty with her hair down again and wearing another of her flirty little sundresses and even cuter jeweled sandals.

"Hey, sweetie." He came forward to enfold her in a tight hug. *No bra,* he noted as he pressed her closer to breathe in her fragrant scent.

She shivered, making him realize he was dripping on her. He left without grabbing an umbrella from the stand in the front foyer of his own cottage. "Oops. Sorry, I'm getting you wet," he said as he stepped back.

"It's okay. I'm fine." She handed him a towel with which to wipe the dampness off his hair and skin. "Is it all right with you if we just eat here? I like the rain better when I'm indoors and dry."

He grinned at her wittiness. "Of course. Although, let me warn you about a possible delay in the delivery. I expect many guests will be doing the same, especially those who are in the cottages."

"No problem. Housekeeping replenished my fruit basket and bottled water. I also have nuts and chocolates in my bag, in case those aren't enough. What would you like to order?"

"I'll have chicken *tinola* and pork barbecue with two cups of rice." The hot soup sounded good in this weather. "Hey, do you want me to order for us so they can prioritize ..." He trailed off when she shook an index finger at him.

"*Tsk, tsk, tsk,* Mr. Ryan. I'm sure if you say jump they will ask how high. But unless you're about to faint from starvation, I'd rather they put us on queue according to the time our order arrived than get special treatment because the boss called it in. My *kubo*, my rules." She said it with a raised eyebrow and a chiding tone.

Oops. She told me off, didn't she? "When you're right, you're right." Blake watched her with appreciation as she spoke to room service to relay their dinner order.

He had become so used to getting his way without any opposition, the power had gone to his head. The Filipinos made it easy sometimes. Most were nonconfrontational and too nice for their own good. Krista was exactly who he needed to keep his ego in check.

He finally figured out this morning what she meant when she told him she'd never had a boyfriend. The things he liked about her were the exact same attributes that kept other men, particularly the Filipinos, away. She was tall, lush, outspoken, and smart.

When she came out of her cottage for their scuba diving excursion wearing a Wonder Woman bathing suit, he anticipated fending off unwanted advances from the other divers. The costume was so appropriate on her, showing off her wondrous curves and mile-long legs to perfection. He couldn't help but whistle in appreciation.

To his surprise, none of the local men leered or ogled. At first he thought they'd been inhibited by his presence, but then he heard them make lascivious jokes about a smaller girl who paled in comparison to his Krista in every way.

My Krista? Wow, since when did I become possessive of a woman? Am I getting in too deep, too soon, with Krista? Blake sat down heavily on the sofa. He had never felt equal parts desire and tenderness towards any woman he'd dated. Krista got him rock-hard just by breathing, but she also made him laugh with her quick wit and dry sense of humor.

The attention she paid to the Hollywood actor the other night had made him jealous, though he hid it well. He attended church with her, a rare occurrence to be sure, and he missed her today while she was away from him.

His brothers would laugh their heads off if they found out what was going on in his life. Curiously, these unfamiliar feelings didn't make him want to run. As a matter of fact, they made him want to do exactly the opposite; get close—get really, really close to Krista.

"So, what did you do this afternoon while I was in boring meetings?" he inquired as she joined him on the couch. Her fair skin had tanned, turning a golden color that enhanced her natural beauty. "Whatever it is must have agreed with you because you're glowing."

Krista stretched languidly. The motion raised the hem of her dress to the middle of her thighs and made him hungry for something other than food. "Nothing. I did absolutely nothing," she sighed. A contented smile bloomed on her face.

She straightened and tucked her legs under her, hiding them from his gaze. "When I get back to Makati, I'm going to tell my friends I'll be their slave for a week. No, erase that—for a month, to thank them for this impossibly generous birthday gift."

"Oh yeah, I remember you told me this trip was a gift. What day is your birthday exactly?" he asked, feigning ignorance.

"Would you believe I was born on the Day of the Dead? November 2nd, All Souls' Day. How ironic is that?" Krista laughed. "When everyone's being all sad remembering their deceased loved ones, my family is celebrating my birthdate."

"A Scorpio—ambitious, intuitive, and passionate. That sounds about right." Blake moved closer as he said each word, until she was on his lap with her arms wrapped around his neck. *Who knew attending focus group discussions about zodiac signs could be useful in seduction?*

"What about you? What's your sign?" She played with his hair.

"Capricorn. Christmas Eve—December 24th. I was a poor deprived child who only got one gift for both Christmas and my birthday." He pretended to sulk.

"Hmm, the Goat. Hardworking, family oriented, practical ..." She walked her fingers along his face, pausing at the cleft on his chin. "...aloof and dictatorial. That sounds about right." She jumped away, laughing merrily as he tried to grab her and bring her back down to his lap.

He groaned when he heard a knock on the door. Their food was here.

***

98

Blake kept her laughing throughout dinner with anecdotes about his siblings. He had her in stitches when he told her how he broke his nose—his little sister had punched him in the face for stealing a Snickers bar from her Trick or Treat bag one Halloween. She was only four at the time, and he was fourteen. He proudly told Krista that Darcy was a champion kickboxer to this day. She might be little, but she could literally kick his ass.

Krista's knowledge of his zodiac sign was spot on. *It's time to prove him right with his assessment of mine, especially the passionate part,* she thought with a secret smile.

"Hey Blake, would you like to play a game?" It was still raining, but it was cozy inside the cottage with the air conditioner turned to a comfortable twenty-two degrees Celsius.

"Sure. What do you have in mind?"

"How about poker?" she suggested, keeping an innocent look on her face. She stood up to retrieve a deck of cards from one of the cabinets. The cottage was well-stocked with board games like Chess, Scrabble, and Monopoly, but they didn't suit her objectives for tonight. Blake's expression told her he'd started to get the drift.

"Strip poker?" He put his palms together in the prayer position, mouthing, "Please, please, please."

"You have a one-track mind," she accused, laughing. *He was one hundred percent correct.* "How about we play a modified truth or dare? Loser chooses to answer, pick a dare, or take off an article of clothing. Holder of the winning hand gets to ask a question or suggest a dare." She sat on the floor, putting the wooden coffee table between them. Blake remained seated on the couch. He had already cleared the table of the tea cups.

"I like this game already. I'm all in!" he said enthusiastically.

She dealt the cards and promptly lost the first hand with two pairs and a queen to his straight flush. He gave a grunt of disappointment; she chose truth.

It will be a short game if we both choose to strip every time we lose, she reasoned to herself. Neither of them had many clothes on as far as she could tell. He wore another of his plain t-shirts, shorts, and probably some underwear, while she only had this dress and her panties. She braced herself for his question when she saw a glint in his eye.

"Why me? For your first time. Why did you choose me?"

Because there's no one else I want to be with but you, she thought, but said instead, "I know you will take care of me; make it good."

"But how did you ..."

She held up one finger. "One question only. Please deal."

He lost the second round and to her surprise, chose truth as well. She hadn't prepared a question because she thought he would go for disrobing straightaway.

"Uhm, have you ever been in love?" He'd said on Saturday he was enjoying his single life too much to give it up, but that didn't mean there wasn't anyone he felt strongly about in the past.

"In like, yes; in love, no," he said simply. He must have seen her readiness to ask him for clarification, so he copied her earlier gesture and held up one finger.

She glared at him, then shuffled the deck and dealt each of them five cards. He lost the third and fourth hands in succession and opted to take off his watch and shirt. She lost the fifth hand and kicked off her sandals. He gave a huff when he lost the next hand with a full house, after she showed her four of a kind.

He was down to his boxer briefs while she remained fully clothed. His chest was a work of art, she observed. Chiseled and hard, she itched to touch it. Her eyes moved to his hips and grew huge when she saw he was sporting a hard-on. She only felt it last night, but the visual was so much better than her imagination. The proof of his maleness certainly matched his height and build.

This is it—carpe diem *time*. Krista took a deep breath. She pretended to shuffle the cards but kept the ten, face cards, and ace of hearts at the end of the deck to give herself a royal flush. She drew his cards from the top and dealt hers from the bottom. Blake's jaw dropped as she turned her cards over one by one to reveal the winning hand.

"Truth or dare?" she challenged.

He started to stand and looked ready to take off his briefs, but he sat again, seeing her face. "Dare," he decided.

Krista stood and pushed the coffee table closer to him, stopping when it touched his knees. Keeping her eyes locked on his, she pulled her spaghetti straps down her arms and let the dress fall on the floor.

She crawled on top of the coffee table wearing only her thong panties; her breasts swayed as she advanced. His eyes darkened to almost black as she got closer and closer to him.

When she reached the edge of the table, Krista stopped and rested her hands on her thighs. "The other day when you kissed me, you said you hoped I'm a good student because you were going to teach me about kissing and touching. I dare you to keep yourself from touching me while I show you what I've learned."

She hoped he couldn't see through her false bravado. Her palms were sweaty, and her heart felt like it was going to beat itself out of her chest.

Blake made a show of holding out his arms and placing them one by one behind his neck. The position pushed his hips forward, aggressively displaying his erection to her view.

Krista licked her dry lips. His pose was so blatantly sexy that it was all she could do not to jump on him and devour him right there and then.

Forcing herself to remain calm and keep to her plan, Krista transferred her hands from her thighs to his and shifted her legs to either side of his muscled limbs.

Once settled on his lap, she leaned forward to close the gap between them and touched her lips to his. She bit his lower lip gently to encourage him to open his mouth for her questing tongue. The dark, rich taste of him filled her senses the moment he did. She moaned when he met her thrusts with his own tongue.

As he rocked his hips in arousal, she clutched his shoulders to keep her balance. Krista squirmed to seek closer contact with him, and felt gratified when his erection lengthened even more, jumping to nestle between her widespread legs.

Krista pulled her mouth away from Blake's to rain kisses down his jawline. She gave him a little push. He willingly let himself fall on his back, watching her, his hands still clasped at the back of his neck. She rearranged herself on top of him, keeping their hips fused together, her hands braced on his hard chest.

Copying what he had done the previous night, Krista ran her hands over his chest, noticing his jolt when she touched his nipple. *Hmm, so it really is the same for men and women.*

She leaned down to touch her tongue to his nipple and heard him groan. She peeked at him from beneath her lashes; he watched her with narrowed eyes. *Heat. There's so much heat in that gaze.*

She kept her eyes on him as she bent to lick his other nipple and trace the line of his chest hair with her finger to where it tapered down under his briefs. He jerked once more and started to move his arms from their confinement, as if he wanted to touch her.

Krista moved out of his reach and told him in a smug voice, "Nah-uh, I'm not done yet. It was a royal flush, after all. The winnings have to match the difficulty of that feat."

She squealed in surprise when he bucked his hips and flipped their positions so fast, she found herself flat on her back with him looming over her.

"Difficulty, my ass. You cheated, you little card sharp," he growled.

Chapter Eleven

Pangako [pang-ah-ko] n. – vow.

The sneaky minx dealt from the bottom of the deck, Blake thought with amusement and a whole lot of approval for her daring. *There are no losers here. We're both winners from her machinations.*

Unfortunately for her, he had to wrest back the control. Had she succeeded in her intent to go beyond the petting from the night before, there was no doubt he would have embarrassed himself. *I haven't been Five-Minute Blake in years; I don't plan to reclaim the title ever again, thank you very much.*

"Settle down, you little wildcat. I ought to punish you for that trick you just played." Blake trapped her hips between his thighs and held both of her hands to curtail her squirming. He made sure not to rest his full weight on her. And grinding into her would guarantee his premature explosion.

"But I won't, since I enjoyed your idea of winning," he continued. He would build her up again in a minute, but for now, he needed to slow down his pulse. He went from zero to sixty when she took off her dress and revealed her miniscule thong panties. *She is Eve personified, a temptation I can't resist.*

It was her right to choose the time and setting of their intimate act. Her *kubo*, her rules. If this was the night she had chosen to give herself to him, he would live up to the trust and confidence she bestowed on him. He'd take care of her. She wouldn't regret honoring him with the gift of her innocence.

"I give you an 'A' for that performance," he said, "but it's time to move the lessons from intermediate to advanced. Are you ready?" At Krista's nod, Blake released her hands and stood up, pulling a condom from his shorts' pocket as he did.

He lifted her from the sofa and carried her into the bedroom. He laid her down gently on to the bed. Moving to turn on the bedside lamp, he placed the condom on the bedside table, aware that Krista was watching his every move.

"Are you on the pill, sweetheart?" he asked, joining her on the bed. He ran his hands up and down her arms, making up for the no-touching restrictions of her dare.

"Yes, to regulate my period." He was relieved for the extra layer of protection.

"Well, then we're ready to resume the lessons. As you were." He lay flat on his back and reassumed his earlier pose, his hands clasped behind his head.

Krista moved on top of him. Once she'd settled, she reached for his arms and placed his hands on the curve of her waist. He looked into her eyes and understood that they would do this together—this act of mutual desire.

He raised his head to meet her halfway when she leaned down to fuse her mouth to his. This kiss was hotter than any they had shared, because this time it was a meeting of equals. She truly was a quick learner.

She continued to map his body with open-mouthed kisses, but paused when she reached the waistband of his briefs.

He rolled Krista gently to her back to reverse their positions. He stayed on his side, to have access to her whole body. She tensed as he put his hands on her hips where the panties rode low. He waited until her tension eased, then he pulled the tiny piece of cloth down from her body and onto the floor. He took his fill of her curvaceous figure from her toes to the top of her head and back again.

"You're exquisite, Krista." His mouth took hers once more in a searing kiss. His hand roamed freely over her soft skin, touching everywhere but at the place where they would be joined soon. He needed to prepare her, to make her relaxed and loose.

Taking her hands, he brought them down to the waistband of his briefs as an invitation to rid him of the last barrier to their closeness. She made quick work of it, impatient in her haste.

Once fully naked, he pulled Krista close to align their bodies together, until not even air could fit in between them. "See how well we match, love? Like pieces of a puzzle." He took her hands in his. "Touch me where you want to be touched, baby. Show me what you want so I can give it to you."

Taking him at his word, she reached between their bodies and held his hardness in a steady grip. He groaned as the dreamt-of scenario finally happened. He reciprocated by parting her legs and pressing his fingers inside her where she was hot and wet for him. She was tight, but slick and ready. So very ready.

Blake took Krista's hands off him and reached for the latex, to put it on his erection. His breath caught as she opened her thighs wider, inviting him to take the next step in this dance. She was so sensuous, his virgin. He vowed to take his time, even if it killed him.

"Look at me, baby," he urged as he positioned himself. "I don't want to hurt you. I'll try to be gentle, but I might not be entirely successful. If it gets too much, let me know and I'll stop." He would probably regret making that promise, but he'd do it. For her.

Krista reached up to touch his face. "Blake, I want this. I want us. I hurt that you're hesitating. Please, come to me."

Staggered by her bravery, he closed the small distance between them and kissed her with a tenderness that belied the heat. Lowering his body, he carefully parted the entrance to her depths with his manhood, sliding it inch by inch, until he was all the way in. He heard her gasp of pain and regretted causing it, but he couldn't undo it now. He could only try to make it better for her from this point on.

He stayed still, letting her adjust to his size and get used to the unfamiliar feeling of fullness. The pleasure of being inside her was intense—almost unbearable— and he had to grit his teeth to keep from groaning out loud. He watched her for signs of discomfort or regret, but found none. "How do you feel, baby?"

She opened her tear-filled eyes and nodded. "I feel wonderful, Blake. Please make love with me." His heart ached with tenderness at her show of equal strength and vulnerability. He caught her mouth in a deep kiss and started to move his hips in slow but deep thrusts.

Her pants and whimpers fueled his desire even more. "So soft, so sweet," he crooned as he lavished her breasts with open-mouthed kisses. She raised her legs to clamp behind him, angling her hips in such a way that his every thrust ground against her clit.

When her inner muscles tightened around him and her moans got louder, he increased his pace and held her even closer. "Let go, Krista. I'll catch you. I promise. Let go," he urged, sensing his own orgasm close to eruption. And she did; her spasms triggered Blake's own prolonged climax.

***

So, that's what it was all about. Krista sighed as she watched Blake walk to the bathroom, unashamed of his nudity. Why would he be? His body was magnificent, whether clothed or bare. Not as comfortable, she grabbed the blanket to cover her own nakedness.

Closing her eyes, she considered the wonder of her new knowledge. It was one thing to read about it but another to experience the ecstasy for herself. *No wonder people do it all the time,* she thought with amazement. What she felt the other night was nothing compared to tonight's fulfillment. There was something *more* to having Blake move inside her that kissing and touching alone could not equal.

She opened her eyes when the bed dipped, signaling his return. He held a wet cloth in his hand. "What's that for?" she asked.

"I was afraid there would be some blood."

She took the washcloth from his hand and put it on top of the bedside table. There was no need for it—she had already checked. She was a little sore down there, and tender in other unused muscles, but she felt great. Scooting closer, she gave him a hug. *He is so sweet.* "Thank you, Blake," she whispered, nuzzling his neck.

"For what, sweetheart?" She lifted her face to look at him and sighed when he swept her hair away from her face and brushed a soft kiss on her lips.

"For being gentle with me, for making it good for me on my first time; for fulfilling your promise to catch me," she explained solemnly. "Is it always like that?"

"First, you're welcome. You deserve to be cherished, and it's an honor for me to give you pleasure." He punctuated the statement with another kiss. "Second, is it always mind-blowingly good? Not really. Sometimes it's just a physical release." It was slight, but she felt his hesitation before he added, "Between the two of us? I hope it will always be as good as tonight, or maybe even better."

Even better? Wow! Striving for a light tone, she poked him on the chest. "Well, big guy, we have to put that to the test another time because I'm a bit sore right now."

110

He tensed and sat up to hold her at arm's length, looking her over as if searching for injury. "I thought you said you're all right."

"*Sssh*, relax. I said I didn't bleed," she assured him, calming him down. She pulled him back down on the bed and cuddled in his arms once more. "And I'm really, perfectly fine. I know you tried not to crush me, but you still outweigh me by at least forty pounds. These muscles are hard, you know." She said the last while patting his chest.

He smacked her butt lightly and she let out a squeal. "*Aray!* What was that for?" She glared up at him. It didn't hurt, but she liked to tease him, anyway.

"Aww, poor little baby. Did it hurt? Want me to kiss it better?" He moved as if to do just that; she wrestled with him until he was flat on his back again. The loon laughed so hard that she pinched his side, which made him hoot even more as he tried to evade her fingers. Krista erupted in a fit of giggles herself when he found a sensitive spot at the back of her knees and proceeded to tickle her mercilessly.

"Stop! Stop! I have to pee." She ran to the bathroom, still laughing. She abruptly came to a stop in front of the mirror and caught her breath, seeing the image of the sensuous woman with her mouth opened in shock.

The woman in the mirror had sparkling brown eyes and sexy, tousled bed hair. Her fair skin was aglow with a pink blush that no cosmetic could reproduce. Her naked body was lush and blooming. *She's beautiful! I'm beautiful.* Krista reached out a finger to touch her reflection.

You're a woman now, Maria Krista Lopez, and you look damned good! Shaking her head at her conceit, Krista freshened up and put on her nightclothes — another sexy ensemble provided by her friends.

Is Blake staying the night? She was racking up her firsts with him. First kiss, first orgasm, first lover, and the first man she'd sleep with. She yawned. By sleep, she meant literally to slumber. This had been an eventful day with the diving and the sex. She needed her beauty rest.

When she returned to the bedroom, she found Blake still on the bed. He had turned down the light, put his boxer briefs back on, and—*darn it*—was reading her romance novel. *Busted.*

"So, this is where you got the inspiration for that seduction scene." His eyes twinkled with laughter. "Can I tell you I heartily approve?" *Of course, he would. It was for his benefit, after all.*

Flushing, Krista wordlessly took the book from his hand and returned it to the bedside table. She forgot she had put it there after she came in to get ready for dinner.

She got onto the bed and arranged the blankets around her before she replied. "I like to read. I learn a lot from books." Books were her refuge. She felt deeply hurt when people made fun of her for reading them. They might not have been rocket science, but they made her happy.

Blake must have sensed her changed mood; he moved to close the distance between them, and he took her in his arms once more. "I like reading, too.

And I wasn't ridiculing you when I said I like your book. I really do." He kissed her forehead.

Getting out of the bed, he added, "We may even try page 117 tomorrow, if you like." The odious man then strode across the room as if he owned it. *Which, of course, he sort-of does.*

Making sure Blake could not see from the bathroom, Krista quickly opened the book to the page he'd mentioned. She blushed again when she read what was going on there. *Hmm. Oh yeah, I like.* Blake bringing her to orgasm with his tongue was something she looked forward to trying, now that she knew how good making love could be.

She closed the book and smiled. She did it. *Congratulations to me. I've fulfilled my Turning-Thirty Vow. I did it!*

TUESDAY

Chapter Twelve

Pagkain [pag-ka-een] n. – food.

She's still sleeping. Blake shook his head, smiling at the sight of Krista sprawled across the king-sized bed.

Even on the island he woke up at six in the morning. His body clock demanded it naturally. He had gone back to his cottage, drank coffee, had a run, showered and changed into fresh clothes, ordered breakfast to be delivered to Krista's kubo, and returned. All within the two hours since getting out of the bed they had shared.

Blake sat on the edge of the bed, contemplating the significance of that. He had never literally slept with anyone. Not once had he invited anybody to his condo; he preferred to go to a woman's place or a hotel so he could leave after having sex. Krista had broken every rule in his book, and he let her get away with it.

When she asked if "it" was always good, his heart stuttered within his chest. A lot of times in the past it was just a quick fuck. He always made sure his partner reached pleasure first, but every single time it was so he could orgasm himself. *No, until Krista, I have never made love with a woman before.*

A moan from the bed broke him out of his thoughts. *Princess Slugabed is waking up.* He decided to aid the process by walking his fingers leisurely along one foot then caressing a shapely calf. He stopped to linger at the back of her knee, which he found to be extra-sensitive last night.

She moaned again, and the sexy sound went straight to his groin. *Oh, that would not do.* She was still very sore. No way would he sport a boner the whole day long without satisfaction.

He climbed on the bed, pulled the blankets off her, and loudly called out, "Wakey, wakey, Sleeping Beauty."

She woke up with an indignant squeal. "Noooooo! Go away." She curled up on her side and put the pillow over her head, attempting in vain to go back to sleep.

He laughed at her childlike behavior and moved closer to take her in his arms. "Come on, sweetie. It's beautiful outside. The sun is bright, and the birds are chirping." He sang out, "Whatever happened to Ms. *Carpe Diem*? We miss her."

That brought her out of hiding. "Ugh. I don't like you anymore." She pouted. Her actions belied her words, because she snuggled closer to him, pillowing her head on his shoulder.

"Why? Don't you like my singing voice? Tralalala." He enjoyed teasing her and making her laugh.

"No. Why are you super cheerful so early in the morning? It's unnatural." She stretched, and he noticed her wince when she straightened her legs. *Poor baby needs a massage.* He would arrange it for later today; maybe get one himself.

They'd take it easy this day, and save the jet skiing and parasailing for tomorrow with Aidan and Maddie. That should be a fun way to celebrate her birthday.

And Aidan's, too. He'd forgotten tomorrow was his brother's birthday as well. He was so focused on Krista, he hadn't realized the significance of his brother's desire to come down to Boracay on that date. But that wasn't until tomorrow; today was still for Krista. And although last night's events advanced the timeline slightly, he still planned to get her into his bed and wake up with her the day she turned thirty.

Obviously waiting for his answer to her question, Krista poked him on his chin dimple. He held her hand and gave it a kiss. Bringing her face up close to his, he said, "How can I not be happy? I have a gorgeous woman in my arms."

He bent to kiss her, but she shook her head and covered her mouth. At his puzzled look, she said in a muffled voice, "Morning breath." She disentangled herself from his hold and took off for the bathroom.

He laughed after her retreating back, but he truly didn't mind. To him, she smelled sweet and felt soft and warm.

He'd woken up with a hard-on. It wasn't helped by the sensation of her supple bottom cheeks cradling his erection so perfectly. That was what drove him out of bed and into a vigorous run at the beach.

He heard a knock at the door and got up to let the servers in to set up their breakfast at the cabana. He hadn't exaggerated when he told Krista it was a beautiful day. Yesterday's rains made everything glisten and shine.

After tipping the waiters generously, he made coffee from the single-serve machine that was part of the amenities in all the rooms at Perlas. The cottages had more advanced brewing systems and a larger variety of flavored pods. He noted that Krista's pod container held flavored creamers, so he prepared a mug for her, guessing on the combination.

He smiled in amusement when she headed straight to the coffee maker as soon as she came out of the bedroom. *My Krista is not a morning person,* he grinned into his cup.

She seemed momentarily confused that there was coffee ready for her; she sipped cautiously and sighed to find it to her taste. Giving him a smile of gratitude, she mouthed, "Thanks."

He led her out to the garden where their breakfast waited. She stopped in her tracks when she saw the food spread out over two tables. There was pork *tocino, longganisa,* beef *tapa, bagnet,* corned beef, *danggit,* garlic fried rice, and sunny-side up eggs. Also included in the spread were *ensaymada, pan de sal,* bagels, pancakes, and waffles. To drink, there were juices and icy water.

She looked at him, her eyes wide in wonder. "Is anybody else joining us? This can feed an entire army." She picked up a plate and got a little of everything.

"It's just us, but I noticed you haven't had a good breakfast since you arrived in Boracay. Saturday was too late, on Sunday we went to church early, and yesterday was rushed because of the scuba diving lessons." He struggled to keep his balance when she set her plate down, rushed up to him, and gave him a hug.

She peppered his face with kisses, saying, "Thank you, thank you, thank you!"

He laughed and patted her on the back. He loved her appreciation of his simple gifts and couldn't wait to give her the rest of his presents. "You're welcome. Now, let's eat."

***

Aww. How could Blake know me so well already? A gift of diamonds wouldn't have pleased her more than feeding her such a sumptuous breakfast. For that reason alone, she'd forgive him for re-arranging her schedule again.

The jet skiing and parasailing were moved to Wednesday, and now they were at the spa, awaiting their couple's massage. She didn't argue, because it made a whole lot of sense.

It took them the better part of two hours to work though half of what he ordered. By the time they finished eating, they were extremely full; they mutually decided that water sports were too strenuous, the weather was sweltering, and moving was overrated. So, they lazed on the sunbeds, talking

118

and getting to know each other better. Krista grinned at some of their exchanges.

> Krista: "What kind of music do you like?"
> Blake: "Hard rock. The louder the better."
> Krista: "Ugh! You'll go deaf before you turn fifty. I adore musical theatre and movie soundtracks."
> Blake: "What about movies?"
> Krista: "Duh! Disney cartoons and romantic comedies, of course."
> Blake: "Of course. Action-adventure for me. I also like the old eighties classics."
> Krista: "Me, too. I'm not very fond of the remakes, though. Do you like the latest Superman? You resemble him, you know?"
> Blake: "Really? I don't see it. He's all right. A bit wooden. Christopher Reeves is still the best Superman for me."

They did move after a while to let the servers clear the food away and to schedule their massage. They also walked to the spa, which was at the other end of the cottages.

Truthfully, after the previous evening and this morning, she would pretty much forgive his bossiness if it was for her benefit. Last night was everything she had read about and more. She took the initiative and felt good about it. She shook her head. No, better than good. *I feel powerful.*

As she promised herself, Krista had examined her conscience since she had done the deed. Her decision to give herself to Blake before marriage held no regrets. How could she be ashamed of something so beautiful—so natural? *May the Lord forgive me, but I will not allow myself to feel sorry.* She might've been guilty of the sins of lust and fornication, but she wasn't penitent at all.

"Ms. Krista? The therapy room is ready now. We're sorry to keep you waiting." The spa attendant had approached without her noticing. Krista waved away the apology and followed the attendant out of the women's lounge, where she'd changed into a robe with a disposable pantie under it.

Krista loved getting massages. Even before she could afford them, she went to the spa because her friends gave her gift certificates either for her birthday or Christmas.

"Sir Blake is already inside. Your therapists will join you shortly. We hope you enjoy your massage treatment." The attendant smiled at her and left. *Did she just wink at me?* Krista frowned, unsure what to make of that, if it was truly a wink and not simply a facial tic.

She opened the door and found Blake wearing a robe like hers. She wondered if the guys also got disposable underpants. Maybe she'd peek when Blake turned over on his front later. She smiled at the naughty thought. Blake raised an eyebrow in inquiry at her smile, but she just shook her head and waved hi.

The couple's therapy room was a stand-alone hut, perched on top of a rock. On one side was the cliff, on another was a view of the sea. The third side faced another therapy hut, and the entrance was through a garden. The sea-facing side had a bamboo wall that could be opened completely during fair weather or closed when it rained. Today, it was open with a canopy of white curtains to keep the sun out of their faces.

Two massage beds, covered in the standard white sheets, took up the middle of the room with enough space between them for two therapists to walk around or stand side by side. Soft music played from hidden speakers, too quiet to drown out the sound of the waves. The gentle breeze from the sea fanned the warm air around them and spread the fragrant scents of lavender and mint throughout the room. The tension in Krista's body started to disappear as soon as she breathed in the scented air; the ambience soothed her instantly.

Krista took off her robe and climbed onto the bed to lay face down. She turned her head to watch Blake as he copied her move, to get into position before the massage therapists' arrival. He wore black briefs like her boy shorts. *Nice.*

A quiet knock signaled the arrival of their therapists—two middle-aged ladies of short stature and muscular build. At the spa reception area, she and Blake had filled out questionnaires to indicate their preferences on the kind of treatment they wanted, what type of essential oil, the amount of pressure, and which points of concentration on the body. Krista opted for the local *Hilot*—the ancient Filipino art of healing.

The ladies got to work at once without a word. She usually liked the masseuse to take a long time on her shoulder and neck areas, but today, Krista specified that she should linger on her lower back and upper thighs. *Oh yeah, it was a brilliant idea to have this done today.* She already felt a thousand times better than she had when she woke up.

When the masseuse signaled it was time to turn over, she was startled to hear a soft snore to her right. She shared a quiet laugh with the ladies. Blake slept soundly on his massage bed. His masseuse looked proud of herself for doing an excellent job of relaxing such a tall and built guy like him. Krista gave her a thumb up sign.

The gesture seemed to break the ice, because the ladies started talking to her. In hushed tones, they remarked in Tagalog, "Ma'am *kayo po pala ang* girlfriend *ni* Sir Blake. *Ang swerte nyo naman.*" You're very lucky.

"He's not only handsome, but also generous to the staff."

Krista smiled at them and closed her eyes, unwilling to engage in a conversation she wasn't comfortable having. The ladies got the meaning behind her silence and went back to their work.

Am I Blake's girlfriend? Yes, as of last night they were lovers, but being his girlfriend meant there was a commitment for exclusivity that they hadn't quite made yet.

Krista must have tensed up; the masseuse touched her shoulder gently, to nudge her into relaxing her muscles. She exhaled deeply, then told herself to stop the negative self-talk and get back to the state of Zen she was experiencing before Blake's snore interrupted it. It worked. She could tease Blake about his snoring later. Right now, it was enough that it brought the smile back to her face.

Chapter Thirteen

Ligaw [lee-gao] v. – to court.

Blake stood outside Krista's cottage, a bouquet of purple calla lilies in his hand. They'd agreed to meet at six.

"Blake, I hope you don't mind if I take a nap," Krista had said when they arrived back at her cottage after the spa. "By myself," she'd added apologetically. "Your snoring through your massage made it impossible for me to fall asleep during mine," she joked cheekily.

He had laughed and agreed, as he needed the time to complete his plans for their dinner date. And this time, it was a date as far as he was concerned.

He'd researched online for the best flowers to give her. Once he found the perfect blooms, he'd had them flown to Boracay on the earliest flight this morning. The rushed delivery and the rarity of his choice had cost him extra; he didn't mind paying it, especially if she liked his offering.

Blake didn't want to present her with roses, because he'd given those to other women. Krista was worthy of something more special, more out of the ordinary.

He learned that the calla lily symbolized beauty, and that fit Krista perfectly. To him, she was undeniably gorgeous. While he liked the meanings behind the white and pink varieties—innocence and appreciation—he thought the purple suited her best. Purple denoted passion.

More importantly, the calla lily represented a major transition, rebirth, or marking a new beginning. Truth be told, the flowers were significant for them both in all those aspects. Krista was not the only one seizing the day; he was, too.

When she opened the door, he congratulated himself again for the rightness of his choice. Krista was a goddess in her white Grecian-style maxi dress with a gold braided belt knotted at the waist, and a pair of matching sandals on her feet. She looked awestruck by the bouquet he held in his hand.

"Good afternoon, Ms. Lopez," he said. "These are for you."

"They're stunning, Blake." She accepted the bouquet with one hand and reached up to touch his face with the other. She lifted herself up on tiptoes to press a light kiss on his lips. "Thank you."

"You're welcome." He smiled widely, pleased by her response to his present. She clutched the bouquet in front of her chest and, although they had no scent, buried her nose in the long petals. *Has she never received flowers before?* "Do you like them, sweetheart?"

"I love them," she said earnestly. "No one has ever given me flowers before. These make up for all those times when I didn't get any, so thanks again."

Her smile was so radiant, he couldn't help but step closer to give her a one-armed hug, careful not to crush the flowers.

"I'm glad," he said, meaning it sincerely. "You're a woman who deserves to receive beautiful things, and I'm happy to give them to you."

He raised her chin and gave her a soft but fiery kiss. She blushed prettily when they parted. Since she didn't seem to want to let go of the flowers, he took her other hand and escorted her out to the beach, where the staff had set out a temporary gazebo outside his cottage.

"Blake, this is incredible!" she exclaimed when she saw the romantic setting.

The staff had outdone themselves. They assembled a domed wicker gazebo with wispy curtains that fluttered lightly in the wind. The rattan finish and dark gold trim of the panels matched the outside walls of the cottages. Inside the canopy were two brown wicker chairs with gold cushions. A glass-top pedestal table held two champagne flutes beside a wicker-covered chiller, which contained a bottle of Veuve Clicquot.

She turned to him in wonder. "What's all these? The breakfast this morning, the spa, the flowers, and now this?"

"Happy birthday, Krista." As she started to protest, he pressed a finger on her lips. "I know, technically it's not until tomorrow, but I want to pamper you today." *And every day if you'd let me.* The thought popped into his mind. *Whoa! Where did that come from?*

Shaking his head, he continued. "If you remember, my brother is coming tomorrow. Even though I hate to leave you, I should spend some time with him. I haven't seen him since his promotion. And, I forgot to tell you that November 2nd is also Aidan's birthday. Today, I want it to be all yours. Okay?" *And I'm not even telling you about Maddie. Four is more than a crowd—it'll be a freaking party.*

She nodded. "Okay. But you've gone to so much trouble. I'm not used to being spoiled like this."

"It's no trouble at all." He knew from their conversations that she'd grown up poor. Only in the past couple of years, since her financial situation improved, had she finally afforded the luxuries she was deprived of for most of her life.

While his family wasn't rich, they'd had a comfortable life. His position in the company and the investments he made over the years had given him a lifestyle most people envied. With no responsibility other than to himself, Blake had amassed a personal fortune that made him quite a catch for any marriage-minded female.

That Krista wasn't pursuing him for his wealth was one of the things he loved about her. *Love? Is that what this is?* Looking at Krista's glowing face, he decided to table the deep thoughts until he was alone to process them. Right now, he had a birthday girl to pamper.

***

Krista leaned back on the couch in Blake's *kubo*, her head spinning. Not just from the champagne, but also from Blake's heated kisses and caresses. After a heavy make-out session, he had gone to his room for some mysterious reason and told her to stay put.

They had finished dinner and moved her birthday celebration into his cottage with the half-full bottle of champagne. It had gotten so dark outside, not even the tiki torches and candles were enough to provide the faintest illumination. Blake had thanked the staff and asked them to break down the temporary gazebo.

Krista felt overwhelmed with the attention Blake had lavished on her. It was like he was courting her. He didn't have to do that. She had already slept with him and would likely do so again tonight, and every night until their return to Makati.

Their dinner was highly extravagant—fresh oysters on the half-shell for their appetizer; Caesar salad, filet mignon, and grilled lobster with in-season vegetables as the entrée; then crème brûlée for dessert.

Blake certainly took note of their conversation on Saturday night during their not-a-date dinner. He'd asked her to describe her ideal date food, and tonight he'd delivered exactly what she wanted. No wonder he was so successful—he paid attention to details and had a phenomenal memory.

"Baby, I have something for you." Blake had returned from his room, hiding something behind his back. "I hope you'll like it." He sat down beside her and handed her a square box wrapped in red foil with a gold ribbon.

Puzzled, she tore into the package. What she saw inside the box made her blush a deep red—books by one of her favorite romance novelists. It was the same author of the book she had in her nightstand, which she'd felt so defensive about with Blake. She hadn't read the titles in her hand, because this series was the writer's first foray into erotica. Krista liked the still-sexy-but-tamer versions better. She regarded Blake, who was waiting for her reaction. "Where did you find these?"

"They were selling them at the *Sari-Sari* store," Blake replied, naming Perlas' sundry shop. Taken from the Filipino term for the neighborhood variety stores that were ubiquitous in the country, it was a decidedly humble name for such an upscale establishment. "Those are the only copies. I lucked out when I was searching for something to give you for your birthday. Do you like them?" He looked at her hopefully.

"Uhm ... yeah ... Thanks. I'm sure I'll read them sometime ..." She broke off when he burst out laughing. "What?" she demanded. *What's the joke?*

"You should see your face. It's so red. I thought you said you love reading." She raised her fists to thump him in the chest, but he raised his hands to block her. "Goodness, woman, you are so violent," he said teasingly, laughter still ringing in his voice.

Grabbing the champagne bottle, he stood and held his hand out to her. "Come, I'll show you my real gift. I left it in the bedroom."

The man had an infuriating sense of humor. Taking his hand, she rose from the couch. She gave him another puzzled look when he handed her the champagne and reached for the discarded books.

"Research material," he said and winked at her. She couldn't help but laugh with him. *He is incorrigible.*

Krista was still smiling when she suddenly came to a stop at the threshold of Blake's bedroom. On top of the white sheets sat a gold box with the signature of a famous shoe designer etched on it. She barely noticed as Blake caught the champagne bottle when she let it fall from her hand in her astonishment.

"Go ahead, open it. I promise it's real this time," Blake said solemnly. She looked up at him and saw that he was serious: nervous, even. That was not the cause of her unease.

She approached the bed and sat down on the edge, staring at the gift. Whatever was inside the box would be the most expensive thing she'd ever owned. These shoes sold for hundreds—even thousands of dollars. She felt stunned at the thought of owning something with a value that could feed so many starving people in this country.

Guilt and greed warred inside her. Blake had his back turned to her, his hands in his pockets, head down. Her heart melted. She was making this proud man feel bad with her hesitation. *It's a gift, Krista,* she scolded herself. *An overly extravagant one, but a thoughtful gift made because he wants to please you. Accept the present, say thanks, and just contribute to charity later to appease your conscience.*

She reached for the gold box and placed it on her lap. "Blake," she called out, imploring him to turn around. When he did, she said, "Thank you. I've always wanted to have something like this. It's extremely generous of you."

"You're welcome, sweetheart. Open the gift. I really hope you like them."

Taking a deep breath, she opened the box and gasped. Inside, she found a pair of red suede Christian Louboutin pumps with pointed toes, ankle straps, stiletto heels, and the signature red leather sole. She took them out of the box and held them lovingly, her fingers caressing the supple material.

She'd been drooling over these shoes for months, whenever she saw them in magazines and on the Internet. She never had any hope of affording them. The patent leather copy she bought from Marikina, the Philippines' primary shoemaking district, was a poor substitute for the real thing.

Eager to see how they fit, she put them on. *Hmm. They feel so good on my feet. But, can I walk in them? That's the real test, isn't it?* She stood up and promptly bumped into Blake.

Chapter Fourteen

Regalo [rə̀-gā-lō] n. – gift.

Seeing her wearing his gift turned Blake on so much that he couldn't wait anymore. He closed the space separating them. He had to have her, right now.

"They are perfect on you, sweetheart." He gazed at her face instead of her feet. With the heels on, she was almost as tall as he. "Do you know why I got you these?"

Krista shook her head.

"The first time I knew I wanted you was when I saw you wearing a pair of red heels under your boring navy pantsuit."

He turned her towards the mirror in the bathroom and stood behind her. "That was when I realized that underneath the conservative librarian exterior was an alluring temptress, secretly craving to burst out."

He untied the knot at her waist, then drew the zipper down the side of her dress. It fell with a whoosh around her feet. She started to step out of it, but Blake was faster—on his knees before she could move. He lifted her feet one at a time and picked up the dress to throw it in the direction of the sofa.

Clad in only a flesh-colored thong and the Louboutins, Krista shivered as he touched and kissed his way up her body, from her ankles to the back of her knees, and on each round cheek of her buttocks. Each pass of his hands was followed by the heat of his lips, wherever they touched. He licked his way up her spine until he was standing behind her again.

He gathered her hair in one hand and raised her hands to clasp its heavy mass on top of her head. The position caused her breasts to jut out in front of her, a sight he spent minutes to savor.

"Gorgeous," he purred. Keeping his eyes on hers in the mirror, he pressed open-mouthed kisses along her neck and shoulders. His hands cupped her breasts, his fingers pulled at her tight nipples.

Krista moaned. "Blake ..." she breathed out. He heard the need and frustration in that one word.

"*Sssh*, baby. This is still part of my birthday present to you. Let me make you feel good." Blake finally turned her around. "I love these heels on you. They align us so perfectly." Then, and only then did he merge their mouths in a long kiss.

Krista made a small sound of protest as Blake ended their kiss, but it was only for a moment as he lifted her in his arms and carried her the short distance to the huge bed. He laid her down gently and stood to strip off his clothes.

He paused when he saw Krista raise her hips to take off her last piece of clothing, leaving her fully naked to his impassioned gaze.

"Baby," Blake rasped. "Please don't take off the shoes. You look stunning in them." He peeled off his pants and briefs in one quick motion and walked to his dresser to retrieve the champagne bottle.

He turned back to see Krista watching him, admiration and desire apparent in her gaze. "Do you like what you see, sweetheart?" He wasn't vain about his looks, but he loved to think Krista wanted him as much as he wanted her.

"You are magnificent, Blake," she whispered, her voice husky with need. "I got lucky when I chose you to be my first lover."

Her words went straight to his cock, getting him ready to claim her once more. But first, he needed to worship her as he'd promised. Bottle in one hand, he knelt in front of her. With the other, he reached for her ankles and pulled her towards the edge of the bed. A pretty blush suffused her face and her creamy skin as he parted her legs to reveal her female flesh, already glistening with moisture.

"Remember what I told you last night about page 117?" He poured the champagne slowly over her breasts and stomach, and watched the still-cool liquid flow down her body into the crevice between her parted legs, shimmering brightly against her neatly trimmed curls. "This is my version."

He kept his eyes on hers while his index finger followed the path the liquid took, all the way down to her cleft. Seeing her close her eyes, he demanded, "Look at me, baby. Watch how I adore you."

His first taste of her quivering flesh was glorious. Sweet, so mouthwateringly delicious. Spurred by Krista's incoherent cries, he flattened his tongue and delved deeper into her softness. He ignored the sting of pain in his scalp when she pulled his hair, as he sucked on the sensitive little nub between her legs and curved his fingers against the wall of her sex. A sense of triumph filled him as

Krista shouted her climax, loud enough to deafen him for a second.

Blake allowed her a few minutes to recover before standing up and donning a condom.

"Did you like that, baby?" At her nod, he said, "We've barely started. There's more. So much more."

He lifted one of her legs and placed it over his shoulder, then surged into her with one quick thrust. Although her channel was slick with desire, it was still tight. He gentled his thrusts, realizing this was only the second time she had welcomed anyone into her body.

Krista squirmed on the bed, her hips meeting his thrusts. "Blake ... please ... harder ... faster ..."

"I don't want to hurt you." He brought her leg down and moved closer to kiss her softly.

"You won't. You can't. Just love me, Blake. Please." Krista raised her hips again, her sex clenching around his flesh.

That was the only invitation he needed. He thrust into her faster, his tight leash on his control broken. Wrapping her legs around his back, Blake plunged them headlong into ecstasy.

***

It was even more mind-blowing the second time around. Krista sighed, clutching one of the pillows to her chest. She grimaced when it stuck to her champagne-soaked skin. *Eww! I need a shower, but Mr. Fastidious is already there.*

He'd invited her to share it earlier, but she drowsily pushed him away. His tuneless singing woke her up and got her thinking of him and of their intense lovemaking.

She gave a full-body shimmy on the bed. A startled laugh burst out of her when the heel of her new shoes snagged on the bedsheets. *I'm still wearing the Louboutins!*

Oh no! Poor Blake's back might be hurting right now. She must have dug her heels into his back a few times while in the throes of passion. *Wait!* She sat up abruptly, almost tumbling in her rush. *He's not supposed to give me shoes as a gift.* Superstition forbade it.

Krista jumped from the bed and ran for the living room. She grabbed her phone from her purse and went online to search for what people believed would happen when shoes were given as gifts. She breathed a sigh of relief when she discovered that the bad luck could be reversed with a symbolic gesture.

"Krista!" Blake's bellow made her dash back to the bedroom. *Is he hurt?*

"What's wrong?" He was putting his clothes on.

He dropped his pants back on the floor and enfolded her in a tight hug. His heart was beating fast. "I thought you left. I don't know why I would think that, but when I didn't see you on the bed, I panicked and was about to run after you to bring you back."

Something like a pinch touched her heart at the emotion she heard in his voice. Running her hands up and down his back, she said, "I'm here. I'm not going anywhere." She stepped back and led him to the bed. He sat down, and she stepped between his legs. Opening her balled-up fist, she showed him the coin in it. "I just went out to get this."

"What's this?" Blake moved backwards on the bed and lifted her to sit on his lap.

"It's my payment for the shoes." At his baffled look, she explained. "They say when you give someone shoes, you're granting them permission to walk away." He shook his head, negating that idea.

She touched his mouth to silence his protest. "To counter that, I have to give you something to make it look as if I'm buying them from you." She beamed at him. "The best one peso I have ever spent in my entire life."

Blake looked stunned, the reaction incongruous with her statement. After a moment, he cupped her face in his hands and kissed her. "I love you, Krista."

Krista froze, her eyes wide in surprise at the fervent declaration.

"I desire you, and I love you. I want to have more than one week with you."

"Blake … I …" She didn't know what to say. She wasn't expecting this. She didn't know how she felt. *I'm not ready.* Tears pooled in her eyes and fell down her face from all the emotions that coursed through her.

"Hey hey, Krista. Sweetheart, I didn't mean to make you cry." Blake tenderly brushed away her tears. "I told you because that's how I feel."

He raised her trembling chin to get her to look at him. She read disappointment in his eyes, along with kind understanding. "You don't have to say anything back right now. I know I'm going too fast for you. I can wait until you know how you feel. When you do, I hope you'll tell me honestly."

What's wrong with me? Why can't I say it back? "Oh Blake! I like you a whole lot, and I want you like I have never wanted another. I gave you the coin because I don't want to walk away from you."

She clutched his shoulders. She had to make him understand. "But I don't know if what I'm feeling for you is love. This is all new to me. You are the first and only man who has ever made me feel this way." *God, I need Maddie right now. I'm so confused.*

"Krista, baby, that's good enough for me." He kissed her again. "No more tears, all right?" She sniffed and nodded. "Can I introduce you to my brother as my girlfriend?"

"Yes, I would like that," Krista replied with alacrity, her tears gone. She had to tell *M'amie* she finally had a boyfriend. She hugged him, overflowing with joy. "I have a boyfriend. It only took thirty years. Best birthday ever!"

Her smile fell when she realized she should also tell her parents, and introduce her first boyfriend to them. Her American boyfriend. But not yet. Not until she was sure of her feelings for him. It would be a battle to get her mom to approve of Blake. If she wasn't one hundred percent convinced herself, how could she fight for him ... for them?

Krista stilled when she felt Blake's manhood stirring beneath her. *Again? He's insatiable.* A wicked smile lit up her face. She moved to get off him and off the bed.

"Where are you going?" he called out, puzzled.

Found them! Turning around from the dresser, she showed him the books he gave her. Maybe she wasn't sure about loving him, but she was absolutely certain about wanting him.

Throwing the books on the bed, she said in her most seductive voice, "Let's do some research."

WEDNESDAY

Chapter Fifteen

Kapatid [ka-pa-teed] n. – sibling, used for both
brother and sister.

Blake woke up to the sound of pounding on the door.
What the fuck? He grabbed his watch from the
bedside table and saw it was eight in the morning. So
much for his internal clock waking him up at six. He
would bet his BMW Maddie was making that racket
outside. His brother wouldn't have been as impatient.

He felt a foot slide along his calves, followed
by a low moan. His birthday girl was waking up.
They wore each other out last night trying out the
lovemaking scenes in Krista's erotic novels. Some of
the positions described in them were so ridiculous,
they laughed more than they made love.

Blake's eyes clouded over with
disappointment when he remembered what else
happened the previous night. *I said, "I love you," but
she didn't say it back.* He got it, though. While he had
been in enough casual relationships to know the
difference, she had no basis for comparison. He'd
have to give her time to process what she felt for him.
Time, yes, but not distance. He resolved to stay close
while she set about making her decision.

Still ignoring the noise outside, he waited for
Krista to open her eyes, then he swooped down to
plant a hot kiss on her surprised mouth. He didn't

allow her to run away from his morning kiss this time.

Her response was instant and oh, so sweet, meeting his tongue's passes with her own. He wished he had more time, but he reluctantly ended it with a quick nip of her lower lip. "Happy birthday, love." She smiled shyly and moved to nuzzle his neck, until the strident banging of fists against wood startled her.

"What's that noise?" Krista pulled away, alarmed. Before he could respond, she jumped from the bed to look around for her clothes. His sexy lady was starting to get comfortable in her own skin. She'd slept naked in his arms for the first time.

She found her panties but not her dress, so she put on one of his t-shirts. Her legs were so long, his shirt only reached mid-thigh, but it covered the most essential parts. She stopped her frantic search and looked at him for an answer. She was absolutely gorgeous with her hair mussed and her lips all plumped up from having been thoroughly kissed.

"It's a surprise," he grinned.

He had also hastily pulled on a t-shirt and a pair of shorts. He took her hand and led her to the side of the front door. Motioning for her to stop, he pulled his shirt down to cover more of her legs. The action only stretched the shirt tighter around her ample breasts. He didn't want his brother to be leering at his woman the first time he saw her, but there wasn't time to do anything about it now.

He swiftly opened the door, jumped back, and put his hands over his ears, fully anticipating the shrieks of joy from the two best friends when they saw each other. Amidst the "Surprise!" "Oh my God!" "Happy birthday, *m'amie,*" and "I can't believe you're here," he nodded to his brother— a signal for him to come in.

"Happy birthday, bro." He smiled and gave Aidan a hug. Even knowing that he was coming to an island, his brother wore a long-sleeved white shirt, and black slacks. With his military bearing and aviator sunglasses, Aidan looked like the poster boy for Air Force recruitment.

They broke off the back slaps when an indignant voice behind him grated out, "It's your birthday today, too?" It was Maddie, looking incredulous at the coincidence.

Blake knew these two would strike sparks off each other. He'd arranged for them to be on the same flights, both incoming this morning and outgoing to Makati the next day. Before Blake could introduce them, Aidan dropped his overnight bag on the floor and approached Krista. Holding out his hand, he said, "Happy birthday, Krista. It's great to meet you."

"Thank you, Aidan. Happy birthday to you, also." She took his brother's proffered hand and shook it firmly. The greeting made her shirt ride up her legs. With a blush, she stepped back to hide behind Maddie, who was still glaring at Aidan.

"Come on, let's go to your cottage," Maddie demanded, obviously in a rush to talk to her best friend.

"Wait, I need to get my stuff. You haven't even greeted Blake yet," she reprimanded her friend gently. She went back to his bedroom to collect his gifts and presumably, her dress.

Maddie was, indeed, being rude. Her face red, she came up to him and grudgingly offered her cheek for him to kiss. "Hi, Blake. How have you been?"

Blake obliged with a peck on her smooth skin. "Hello, Maddie. I've been just peachy. It's nice to see you again." He grinned at her, openly enjoying her unenthusiastic observation of social pleasantries.

"Thanks for keeping my visit a surprise for Krista. I appreciate you making the arrangements for my arrival at such short notice."

He shrugged. "It was my pleasure. I knew she was going to be happy you're here to share her special day."

Now that he and Krista had reached an understanding, he could afford to be indulgent to her closest friend. "How did you know to come here instead of Krista's cottage?"

Maddie put her hands on her hips and raised her left eyebrow. "How long have we known each other, Blake? Two years? Surely you don't expect me not to know your designs on Krista?"

"*Touché*, Mademoiselle Duvall." Blake grinned in acknowledgment of her correct assessment. He checked that his brother wasn't close enough to hear. "So, you didn't come here to cockblock me?"

Maddie frowned. "No. As if I could have stopped you. I'm here for my best friend. I have news that couldn't be told over the phone. I also brought work for you. For the resort."

His jaw tightened at the mention of work. He hated the intrusion of real world affairs into his idyllic retreat. "We'll do it tomorrow. Today, we celebrate Krista's and Aidan's birthdays."

Maddie gave him a typical Gallic shrug. "You're the client."

Damn right I am. He forgot his annoyance when he saw Krista exit his room dressed in last night's clothes. She carried the shoe box, books, and remnants of the calla lilies he gave her for her birthday. They had crushed a few petals during one of their erotic re-enactments.

He approached her and put his arms around her. "I guess I'm going to miss you this morning, huh?" She nodded. *Yup.* He expected this. That was why he had planned yesterday's full day with her. "Do you still want to do parasailing and jet skiing today?" Another nod.

"Let's meet at the clubhouse for an early lunch, say eleven thirty, then head out to the beach afterwards. How does that sound?" Three hours should be enough for their girl-to-girl talk. Maybe Maddie could help her sort out her feelings for him. He hoped so.

"Sounds good," she replied and met his kiss with a sweet smile. "See you later." She included Aidan in the parting acknowledgment, then left with her friend.

***

"You didn't tell me you got a girlfriend," Aidan remarked, heading for the coffee maker.

Arms crossed, Blake replied, "She wasn't mine yet when we last spoke." His brother raised an eyebrow. When they talked on the phone on Sunday he mentioned Krista, but not what she meant to him.

Aidan leaned back on the counter, sipping his coffee. "Fast work, bro."

He knew that was coming. Blake got a mug from the cupboard and made his own brew.

"Not really. We've known each other since May. She works for me."

Blake was prepared for his big brother's censure. The company had a fraternization policy. It was something he had to take a closer look into, moving forward and regarding his relationship with Krista. As CEO, he had everybody in the company reporting to him, even indirectly. But, he was an expatriate; there might be a loophole somewhere he could exploit.

"Hmm, that seems unusual for you. You don't normally date colleagues. She must be special."

Huh? That was unexpected, but he'd take it. He had enough stress about being possibly accused of favoritism—or even worse when he promoted her, sexual harassment—without worrying what his family thought of the situation.

If word of their relationship got out, Krista could be subjected to gossip and drama among the female staff. Right now, she was well-liked and respected by her colleagues, but that was because she'd deliberately crafted an image of untouchability.

Will she go back to wearing her conservative outfits and hiding her physical assets? Or will she live up to her new motto of carpe diem*?* He didn't have any answers at the moment, and that bothered him.

"She *is* special. Krista is beautiful and sexy, but more than that, she's exceptionally intelligent—maybe smarter than me." Another raised brow. That brow was getting a lot of exercise this morning.

"That's high praise, coming from you. You're no slouch in the brains department."

Neither was Aidan. All the Ryan children had high IQs, especially Darcy, who was in the genius level. "Is there anything wrong with this paragon? Are you sure she's not only after your money to get her family out of poverty?"

Blake didn't like his brother's insinuation. His jaw tightened. "Bro, be careful what you say about my woman. Krista is not a gold-digger."

Aidan held up his hands. "Hey, I don't know her, okay. I just want to make sure you do."

Blake's expression relaxed. "I can't say I know her very well already." She hadn't talked about her family much, except to say she was close to them. He knew more about her friends than her parents or siblings. "What I know, I like. It's odd, really. She has plenty of insecurities, but she also has a lot of pride. She's incredibly independent; she looks at my gifts with suspicion." Blake smiled fondly as he recalled the various instances when she demonstrated his next complaint. "And, she's always scolding me when I'm being arrogant."

146

Even knowing it would make him sound too sensitive, he continued. "But, I don't know exactly how she feels about me. She hasn't had a lot of experience with men. I'm her first lover."

He didn't realize how much he would appreciate having his brother here to talk with, regarding this new development in his life. They were close growing up, having been born only fourteen months apart, but their respective jobs—especially Aidan's highly classified one—brought some distance in the past few years.

"And you want yourself to be her last, as well."

Since when did my brother become so understanding? They really needed to get together more often. Craig, too. "Yeah. She's The One, A." *There, I said it.* His brother just nodded his head.

"What are your plans? Are you staying in this country indefinitely?"

His brother's overly casual tone alerted Blake to a possible hidden meaning in his question. *Is that why Aidan is in the Philippines? Is something about to go down in the country that I should be cautious about? The new administration had been making waves in both domestic and international affairs, but things couldn't be that bad, could they?*

"I'll probably go back to the US, eventually. Why? Should I be making any?"

Because of his performance in the Philippine office, Blake could have a plum job anywhere in the world he wanted. He'd considered transferring earlier this year, perhaps to take on a developing market or a regional job, but then Krista came along and he decided to stay. He had seven months to decide whether to ask for another extension or go elsewhere.

"All I can say is that you should always have an exit strategy," Aidan replied cryptically.

Blake sighed in frustration. It was so hard to talk to his brother when he was in his "top secret" mode, but he could always count on Aidan if anything serious happened.

"It could be tricky, since it looks like you're putting down roots in this country. Partnership in an island resort ... the girl ..." *Subtle, bro.*

"The resort is an investment. I could live anywhere, and it will still yield profits for me. The *woman* ..." Blake stressed the word. Krista wasn't a young innocent Miss anymore. "... is strong and feisty. The Filipinos are tough and resilient. They survived a dictatorship and two People Power Revolutions; they'll handle whatever comes next."

He intended to check out his work options this coming Monday, but whatever he did, wherever he went next, he'd take Krista with him.

Aidan straightened and clapped his hand on Blake's shoulder. "She seems to have her hooks dug deep into you, little brother. Be careful she doesn't break your heart."

Blake looked Aidan in the eye. "There's always a first time for everything. Maybe I'll let her." He saw understanding and perhaps a little sympathy there, before his brother's gaze became hooded again.

"Maybe you should. For what it's worth, I like her." Adrian grinned. "She's got great legs."

Blake let out a jealous growl and Aidan roared with laughter. Big brothers are a huge pain in the ass. He decided to do a little needling himself. "So, what happened with Maddie?"

Aidan turned away to wash his mug. "Nothing happened. She arrived late and delayed the flight by fifteen minutes."

Uh-oh. Tardiness was a cardinal sin in Aidan's eyes. Maddie had plenty of sterling qualities, but punctuality wasn't one of them. Her work was excellent, so Blake always forgave her when she came in late for meetings.

But Aidan had no patience for what he considered lack of discipline, even—correct that, especially—in someone as stunningly beautiful as Maddie. "Did she apologize?"

"No," he bit out. "She sashayed onto the plane and waved to the pilots like she's Miss Universe. Then she held out her hand to me as if I should be honored she acknowledged my presence at all."

Blake looked down into his mug to hide his grin. Maddie and Aidan were the only passengers on the flight.

"What did you say to her?" For sure it was something cutting and honest, but unflattering.

"I told her she was late and if she could stop flirting with the pilots, we could take off and finally get on our way." Aidan walked towards the bedroom, finished with the conversation. "Do you have extra sheets? I want to take a nap. I've been up since four."

Ah. Blake got it now. That explained Maddie's irritation with his brother. It was rare that the half-French beauty got rebuffed by any man. *Sounds like a plot of a romance novel.* He sniggered as he followed his brother to show him where they kept the bedding.

Chapter Sixteen

Kaibigan [ka-ee-bee-gan] n. – friend.

They didn't talk during the short walk to her cottage, but Krista knew the moment they entered that Maddie would be on her like a police interrogator.

Once inside, she turned to her friend and said, "Before you question me, Inspector Javert, I need to shower and change clothes. Can you order some breakfast for us? Please? I'll tell you everything later. I promise." She walked to the bedroom before Maddie could respond, knowing that her friend would simmer, but she'd follow Krista's request.

Krista made quick work of the shower, since she and Blake had spent time at the whirlpool the previous night. Granted, they did more lovemaking than bathing, but she felt clean, nonetheless. After donning a sporty bikini set, then covering it with a tank top and shorts, she went out to look for Maddie.

Whenever she had the opportunity, Maddie spent her time outdoors. It made sense that she was out there right now, probably already in her bikini. Maddie was darker than Krista, even though Maddie was considered a mestiza with her mixed French and Filipino heritage. She thrived in the sun, sea, and sand, and Boracay was her happy place.

Krista confirmed her theory when she saw Maddie's t-shirt and shorts on the couch, her overnight bag lay open on the floor. *Ha. Do I know my best friend, or what?*

Quickly grabbing a mug of coffee, she followed her friend to the garden area.

As she suspected, Maddie had moved two chairs to the sunshine; the table and remaining chairs stayed in the shade for Krista. Sitting on one chair, Maddie had her long legs stretched out on the other while munching daintily on her fruit salad. She wore black sunglasses and the tiniest red bikini Krista had ever seen.

Krista was relieved to find bagels and cream cheese on the table, along with a fruit basket containing grapes, mangoes, jackfruit, pomelo, and guava.

Although they were the same height, Maddie looked smaller when they stood side by side; she was slim and elegant while Krista was stacked and curvy. Her bestie kept her model-thin body by working out daily at the gym and eating a low-fat, low-sugar, low-carb diet.

In the past, Krista envied Maddie's body. But after last night, with Blake showing her repeatedly how much he loved her curves, she felt more confident of her own allure.

Reaching for a bagel half, she sat down and prepared herself for the grilling of her life. "So, I finally have a boyfriend." Saying it still made her giddy. "No more NBSB. *Yehey!*" She spread cream cheese on the bread and munched happily.

"Congratulations. I'm happy for you."

Krista raised her eyebrow.

"I am! I can see that you're glowing. Good thing I'm wearing sunglasses, or I'd have been blinded by the smile on your face."

Krista laughed at her friend's exaggeration.

"I take it you've done the deed? Your cherry has been popped?"

Color tinted Krista's cheeks. "Well and truly gone. Ahead of schedule as well. On Monday night. I seduced him."

That statement brought Maddie's feet down from the chair. "You did? *Oh là là!* Way to go! How did it happen?"

Krista reddened even more.

"I didn't mean how, *how.* I meant how did you seduce him?" She removed her sunglasses to peer closer at her.

"Well, it was raining that night, so we stayed indoors. After dinner, I suggested we play truth or dare strip poker, and then I cheated so I could dare him." Her eyes took a faraway look as she remembered their sexy game.

"That's fantastic! I love it that you took control. And you were the one to decide when and where. *Félicitations, m'amie. C'est super.* How was it? Did it hurt?"

Krista blushed again. "It stung at first, but Blake was gentle and patient, and he really took good care of me."

She didn't need to tell Maddie all the details—she was sure her friend knew how it was done. "You know I've been doing splits for dance and yoga, so there wasn't really much tearing or bleeding."

"I told you he's good." At Krista's choked laugh, she backtracked and said, "I mean, I heard someone say he was good."

That sobered up Krista instantly. That was the thing—he wasn't hers first. Who knew how many lovers he'd had before her? He told her he had never been in love, but …

Softly she told her best friend, "He said he loves me, Maddie." She put down her half-eaten bagel. She couldn't take another bite.

"Wow!" There was real surprise on Maddie's face. "What did you say?"

"I didn't say anything. I cried. I'm not sure how I feel." She looked at her friend for understanding. "Blake is so generous. He lavished me with so much attention these past few days. He obviously knew you were coming today, so he celebrated my birthday with me all day yesterday. He pampered me with breakfast, a massage, and dinner. He gave me flowers. Not just any flowers, but rare purple calla lilies. And he gave me a pair of Christian Louboutin heels!

"He's rich, Maddie. Although I'm not poor anymore, I can't even begin to imagine what it's like to just buy a nine-hundred-dollar pair of shoes. Plus, he's my boss. I know he's not my direct supervisor, but he's the CEO. I can't hope for a promotion; otherwise, people will accuse me of sleeping my way to get it, and accuse Blake of favoritism."

Maddie was nodding.

"Then, there's the fact that he's an expatriate—an American. He can leave anytime.

154

What if the company wants him to move to another country? What am I going to do?"

"You thought all these things in the split second after he told you he loves you?" Maddie's voice was filled with incredulity. "Did you tell him any of these?"

"No. But I didn't tell him I love him, either." *Do I?*

"Do you?" Maddie always had the knack of reading what was on her mind.

"I don't know. Maybe. Possibly. I don't have a frame of reference for this kind of feeling. I've only loved my family and you, my friends. I've always had difficulty saying it, even to my parents or to my siblings. Blake is my first lover. How do I know that it's love and not just lust?" *It seems so easy in the books. In real life, not so much.*

"What do you think of Aidan?" Maddie asked, seemingly out of the blue. At Krista's confused look, Maddie explained. "Aidan Ryan, Blake's brother. You met him thirty minutes ago. He has the same birthday as you. He looks a lot like Blake, except that he's more handsome, much sexier, and a thousand times more arrogant."

Krista didn't notice, but it seemed Maddie had. "Excuse me? I beg to disagree. Blake is better looking and much, much hotter than his brother. I don't know anything about Aidan being more arrogant than Blake; my boyfriend is pretty sure of himself. It must run in the family." She smirked at Maddie.

"Aidan just seems to have a stick up his behind with that chin up, chest out, shoulders back, stomach in, posture of his." She wanted to see how Maddie would respond to that. Her best friend seemed strangely hostile towards Aidan.

"That's because he's an officer in the military. It comes naturally to him." Maddie was defending him now.

She shook her head at Krista and started speaking in a big-sister voice. "But that's not why I mentioned him. My point is there was a good-looking man around who could be Blake's twin, but you barely noticed him because you didn't feel anything for him. So, it couldn't be lust, otherwise you would be attracted to Aidan as well." The last sentence was uttered with so much relief that it made Krista smile.

"How do you know I don't find Aidan attractive? I only said he's super formal."

Maddie was glowering at her now. Krista continued to taunt her. "Maybe now that I've had some sexual experience, I could venture into threesomes. What do you think?"

She laughed out loud at her friend's stormy expression. "I'm kidding. I'm kidding." She dodged a bagel that was thrown at her head.

Still laughing, she threw a grape at Maddie's face and she caught it with her mouth. They laughed uproariously.

Sobering up, Krista said, "Seriously, Mads, I don't even know what to do with the one I suddenly have. What would I do with two? You can have

Aidan, I'll keep Blake." She couldn't help herself. Her friend's blushing face said it all.

"But you're right. I don't just feel lust for Blake. Aidan is not the first handsome man I've met and didn't notice, while I was with him. That movie actor from *Thor*—the villain—was here at Perlas over the weekend, and he barely made my heart beat faster than normal." Krista grimaced at the remembered embarrassment with the Hollywood star.

"I truly like and admire Blake. He's more than my match in terms of intelligence. He makes me laugh. He's very decisive with everything. He's not scared of me. Nor does he get mad when I speak out and point out his faults. He takes care of me." She could talk all day about Blake's qualities.

Maddie reached out to clasp her hands. "Krista, *chérie,* I cannot tell you how you feel. Only you can do that. I haven't fallen in love yet, but what you're describing to me sounds very much like it."

She let go of Krista's hands and leaned back in her chair, looking smug. "I know it's rude to say it, but I'll say it anyway—I told you so." She wagged a finger at her friend. "I warned you last Saturday to be careful and not to fall in love with him, and here you go all fallen." Her voice held no censure, just pure empathy.

"Yeah, you did. Your warning fell on deaf ears, it seems." Krista agreed, without much regret.

"I knew it would, even as I spoke it," Maddie replied. "Your heart is ready."

A moment later her smile dropped, and she came over to sit beside Krista. "*M'amie*, have you told Blake about your mom?"

Krista heaved a deep sigh. Her friend had never been afraid of talking about this difficult topic, whereas she would rather not speak of it at all. She had been avoiding any mention of her family to Blake; hadn't reciprocated when he spoke about his own with so much love and affection.

"No," she said, looking away. "This was supposed to be only a weeklong affair while we're here in Boracay. I'd thought Blake only wanted something temporary and we would break up on Saturday morning. Go back to being CEO and subordinate on Monday. I was trying not to hope too much. It was a total surprise to me when he told me he loves me. That he wants more than one week with me."

She faced Maddie. "Everything has been happening so fast. It still doesn't feel real." Frowning, she asked her friend, "Do I really have to tell him now? It isn't as if they'll be meeting anytime soon."

Maddie regarded her for a moment before she replied, "You're right, it's not urgent. But you must make sure to prepare both sides before you spring the news. Otherwise, there'll be hurt feelings. Your relationship with Blake is too new to be tested so early. And don't forget, there's no Drama Mama like a Filipino mom in full guilt-trip mode. You know that." A grimace and an eyeroll accompanied the last statement.

Krista laughed. Maddie and her mother were the opposite of the Gilmore Girls. Ever since she'd known them, they had fought about anything and everything. That was why, even though she hadn't known her father until she was sixteen, Maddie still favored him over her mom.

The chime of bells ringing broke through her amusement. "What's that?"

Maddie was already standing up. "It's my phone. I set the alarm for eleven so we won't be late for our lunch with the Ryan brothers. I don't want to be scolded by Mr. Officer-But-Not-A-Gentleman Ryan twice in one day. Come on, let's go."

Chapter Seventeen

Pares [pa-res] n. – pair.

Damn. Blake was happy he didn't have his brother's job. To be always on one's guard must be very exhausting. Even though he told Krista they would meet at eleven thirty, he and Aidan had been at the clubhouse for fifteen minutes already.

Aidan had chosen a corner table. Sitting in the shadows with his back to the wall, he had a view of all entrances and exits. No one could approach them from any side without being seen.

Even without a weapon, and in a tropical island paradise, Aidan was locked and loaded, ready for action. Despite the casual t-shirt and swim shorts Blake lent him, Aidan still looked exactly like the decorated warrior he really was.

Blake was instantly on alert when he felt his brother tense beside him. He looked around in search of danger but saw only beauty and grace entering the room. Either one of them could make heads turn anywhere they went, but together, Krista and Maddie were an exceptional sight.

Both tall and beautiful, they were the epitome of the twenty-first-century Filipina. Krista, with her fresh face, round curves, and long black hair tied in a simple ponytail had more traditional looks with the Malay, Spanish, and Chinese influences mixing pleasingly in her features.

Maddie was more a representative of the new reality of global citizens the Filipinos had become; curly light brown hair with blond highlights, which was artfully arranged on top of her head; exotically slanted hazel eyes; and naturally plump lips, enhanced by a deep red lipstick that matched the bikini showing through her filmy cover-up.

While Krista turned him on, he could see how Maddie's in-your-face sensuality might entice any hot-blooded man. What she lacked in the chest department, which wasn't much, Maddie more than made up for in the bottom half. As evidenced by the reaction of the server, standing frozen, watching her from behind as she strutted towards the brothers.

Brought up to be gentlemen, they rose from their seats as the women approached. Krista flowed into his arms naturally, as if she was made especially for him.

"Hi, baby." He kissed her on the cheeks, aware of the eyes on them. He wanted to do more, but he was respectful of Krista's reticence in public.

"Did you have a good chat with Maddie?" He pulled out a chair beside him for her. He preferred having her on his lap, but that, too, would have to wait until they were in private.

"Thank you. Yes, we had a nice morning." She eyed her friend and Aidan, who stood staring at each other.

"Ms. Duvall," Aidan said, pulling out a seat for Maddie.

"Thank you, Colonel Ryan." She nodded, sitting gracefully on the proffered chair. Aidan pushed it in and walked back to his seat.

"I appreciate the promotion, but I'm only a lieutenant colonel," his brother corrected her rather curtly.

"Oh, I apologize," Maddie said. Her expression was anything but contrite. Aidan inclined his head in terse acknowledgment.

Blake and Krista looked at each other, amused at the charged back-and-forth.

"Shall we get food?" Blake signaled the server to come and take their order. It was the same young man who couldn't take his eyes away from Maddie's rear end. He noted his brother's dark looks coming from the corner as he stared at the admiring boy, who went straight to Maddie's side.

"I will have a salad with light balsamic vinaigrette dressing and grilled chicken breast— skinless and boneless, no oil, just salt and pepper. I'll also have cold bottled water with a wedge of seedless lemon and mint leaves in a glass. No ice. Thank you."

Blake hoped the awed waiter got all of that. He seemed to be in a trance after Maddie threw a careless smile his way.

Aidan took the boy out of his dream state with a show of clearing his throat. "*Ahem*. Grilled pork belly, rice, and Coke for me. Thank you." No muss, no fuss. The poor waiter looked like he was about to salute. He did stand up straighter when he faced Aidan.

"*Pancit Canton* and iced tea, please. *Maraming salamat.*" The polite request came from his sweet girlfriend, ever so gracious to the waitstaff. He reached for her hand, kissed it, and held it on top of the table. *Surely that's a tame enough public display of affection for the locals.*

"*Sisig* plus additional rice, and San Mig Light, please. Thanks, Edwin."

The waiter bowed his head and left.

Krista turned to her friend as soon as the server was out of earshot. "Maddie!"

"What?" She wore a too-innocent look on her face. "I didn't do anything." She knew very well she'd kept the boy tongue-tied.

"I think, Ms. Duvall, all you have to do is breathe and men will fall at your feet to worship you," Aidan drawled in a deceptively lazy voice.

"Please call me Madeleine, Lieutenant Colonel," Maddie offered. The zinger came all too swiftly. "How flattering of you to say so. Yet you're still in your seat. Why is that?"

"And I would like it very much if you would call me Aidan, Madeleine," he returned silkily. "As to why I'm not kneeling at the altar of your beauty, all I can say is I'm not very religious. The military beat that out of me. It's hard to follow the Ten Commandments when your main job is to kill the enemy." His brother's hard voice was filled with cynicism and weariness.

Before Maddie could respond, Blake cut in.

"Guys, we only have two jet skis, so we have to double up to get to the staging area where the boats

163

and parachutes are parked. We'll do the same with the parachutes. They can only take a maximum of two people." He shook his head. "All the guests seem to want to do the same thing as us today. I'll take Krista, and Aidan will pair up with Maddie."

He held up his hands when the battling duo tried to protest. "Nope. No objections. It's for the safety of the equipment. The weights need to be balanced." He winked at Krista when she pinched his side.

***

Blake stopped the jet ski a few yards from the beach in front of his cottage and lifted Krista off into the knee-deep water. He jumped down behind her in a hurry. Hastily shedding his personal floatation device, he motioned for her to do the same. He hung both vests on the handles, then towed her to the shore at a run.

"Blake, where are we going?" Krista puffed out, lengthening her strides to keep up. "What about Maddie and Aidan?"

"We're going to take a shower. Aidan will take care of your friend."

He opened the door to his cottage. After a cursory stamp of his feet on a mat, he lifted Krista into his arms and carried her inside.

"Blake, we're dripping all over the floor." Krista cupped a hand to her bottom in a failed attempt to catch the water.

"Don't care. It'll dry."

They reached his bedroom and Blake paused to get a condom from his bedside table before taking Krista into the bathroom.

He set her down on the countertop, then turned on the water. Once satisfied with the temperature, he tugged Krista back into his arms and into the shower.

He ravaged her mouth as if he was starving and she was a feast. Krista moaned and met his kiss with equal passion. He loved that she was so responsive to his touch.

His hands roamed all over her body, tugging the strings of her bikini until it came off. She helped by pulling his shorts down, then she held his aching manhood in her palms. *Fuck yes!*

He dislodged Krista's hands from his cock and groped for the condom, putting it on with shaking hands. Wrapping her leg around his waist, Blake dipped two fingers into her heat, to test her readiness. He slid a hand beneath her butt and tilted her hips to receive him.

"I'm sorry, baby. I have to have you now." He removed his fingers and pushed forward, plunging his hardness into her. They gasped simultaneously, at the moment of complete joining.

"Blake … I can't …" Krista breathed out, her limbs trembling. Comprehending that her knee couldn't hold her, he raised her other leg, fully supporting her weight, and anchored her against the wall.

He gripped her hips and set a punishing rhythm, continuing to slide into her slick heat until

Krista's inner muscles clamped on his hard flesh when she came. He followed soon after, becoming rigid, shuddering, and spilling into her.

Reversing their positions, Blake leaned back onto the tiles to catch his breath, his arms still around Krista. When he felt more stable, he separated their bodies so that he could get rid of the rubber. He loved the idea of riding her bareback, but not until Krista was as committed as he was. *Soon.*

She was still shaking with the aftermath of their passion. He adjusted their positions so the shower wasn't raining directly down on her. Reaching for the shampoo, he started washing her hair. "Baby, are you all right?"

She nodded and kissed his chest. "I'm great, honey." *Wow, an endearment. That's a first.*

"I'm sorry I had to rush you like that. If I could've made love to you in the air, I would have done it during our parasailing experience."

He rinsed her hair and got the towel to dry her. "Your utter joy in the ride turned me on so much; I couldn't wait for us to get down so we could do exactly what we just did. I hope I wasn't too rough." He enfolded her in his arms, towel and all.

"I would have said so if you were," Krista reassured him, giving him a quick kiss.

She took a step back and got another towel to wrap around herself. "I couldn't decide which I liked better—the diving or the parasailing. Both were equally amazing." She sat down on the bed to dry her hair more thoroughly.

166

He laughed and dropped a kiss on her forehead. "That's what's great about having a boyfriend who's a partner in a resort. You can do both, anytime you want."

He strode to his bureau to take out a shirt and shorts for her to wear on the walk back to her cottage. When he turned to hand them to her, he was immediately concerned to see the expression of unease on her face.

He crossed the room to her side and took her in his arms. "What is it, sweetheart?"

"Blake, you know I'm not with you because of your wealth, right?" Her eyes pleaded with him to deny the ugly thought.

"Of course, I know that, Krista. You weren't aware that I'm a partner at Perlas until you got here. You even have a tough time accepting my gifts, except for the cheap hats." *What could have brought this on? Did Maddie say something?*

"It's just that people will talk, and I don't want you to think I chose you to become my lover because of what you can give me. I have been providing for myself and for my family for a long time now. I can pay my own way."

She was fierce with pride in her accomplishments. As she should be. They were impressive for someone her age and gender in their industry.

He berated himself for being so careless with his words. He was also learning how to be in a committed relationship.

Hugging her again, he said, "I'm sorry, baby. I didn't mean to make you feel bad. I like giving you things. If it's in my power to give you something I know will make you happy, I'll do it. It's my way of saying I love you."

Krista touched his face and leaned in for a kiss. "I'm sorry, too, for being such a drama queen about this. It's a sensitive issue for me, and the gap between our financial stations is something I should work hard to deal with. Thank you for everything you've given me. You don't have to present me with something every day, you know." She looked at him sternly. "I'll only allow it because it's my birthday, but starting tomorrow, no more, okay?"

She smiled when he nodded; to him that meant everything was good with them again.

He still had one more present for her. Since it was still technically her birthday, he wasn't breaking the promise he'd agreed to just now.

Chapter Eighteen

Kaarawan [ka-ah-ra-one] n. – birthday.

Krista sat bemusedly looking up at the festive balloons and *banderitas* decorating the gazebo at the resort's outdoor restaurant. Blake had gone all out with the preparations for her and Aidan's joint celebration. He was like the Santa Claus of birthdays. She shook her head fondly at the childlike delight her boyfriend took in planning and executing this party for the four of them.

He'd arranged for the *karitelas* again to fetch them from their cottages, more for the benefit of Aidan than hers and Maddie's, because they had been on them before.

When they arrived, there were two chilled bottles of champagne on the table and the chef had prepared a small *Cebu*-style *lechon* especially for them. The highly flavorful roasted pig from the Southern capital of the Philippines was known for its stuffing of spices and herbs, which included lemon grass, leeks, salt, pepper, and garlic. *Lechon* was a staple in every large celebration throughout the country.

All of them drank the champagne, including Maddie who was concerned about the calories in it at first; Krista cajoled her into taking a few sips until she finished a whole glass.

Krista thought she was going to turn permanently red when Blake kept giving her and the champagne heated looks, reminding her of what they did with it the previous night.

Even Aidan was relaxed in his chair and had lessened the frequency of examining his surroundings like he was waiting for an enemy to attack. What increased were the intense looks he and Maddie exchanged when they thought no one was looking.

She grinned in delight as the waitstaff approached the table with a cake bearing two candles, one for her and one for Aidan. To hers and Aidan's amusement, Blake and Maddie launched into a tipsy, offkey version of the happy birthday song.

"Thank you, thank you," Aidan remarked after he and Krista blew the candles out. "That was painful. Please don't do it again." He smiled when he said it.

"You're welcome." Reaching into a bag that a staff member had given him, Blake declared, "I've got gifts!"

Of course he did. Krista groaned. "Blake! I thought we talked about this already."

"Krista, sweetheart, it's still your birthday today, so I'm technically allowed to give you a present." He stared at her with puppy-dog eyes, but with a cheeky smile on his lips.

"Oh okay, but give Aidan's first." *What else could he give me that he hasn't already?*

Blake handed his brother an orange box with black ribbons bearing the name Hermes, the famous French high-fashion luxury goods manufacturer. Inside were a pair of silver cufflinks and a blue silk twill tie. Her eyes widened. *Those are almost as expensive as my shoes.* He hadn't lied when he said giving was his love language.

"Thanks, B." Aidan rose from his chair to give his brother a hug. They were an affectionate family, the Ryans. No sooner had he returned to his seat than he made his excuses to take a call.

"Now, for my baby," Blake announced. He brought out a similar box to last night's gift of erotic books. He laughed when she raised her eyebrow at him. "It's not books again, sweetheart. I promise." He made the Boy Scout sign.

Krista noticed the resort's name on the box; she made a mental note to check out that boutique tomorrow. She hadn't bought thank-you gifts for her friends yet. Opening the lid, she caught her breath at the complete set of cranberry freshwater pearls inside—a necklace, bracelet, and earrings. They were nearly the same color as her Louboutins.

She looked at Blake, who had moved to crouch by her side while she was opening the gift box, and pressed a light kiss on his lips. She didn't care anymore if anybody saw them. "Thank you, Blake. These are lovely."

He returned her kiss and whispered, "Will you wear them for me soon? Just the pearls?"

She reddened, but nodded. She wished it could be tonight, but they both had guests. They'd have to be satisfied with the quick bout of passion they shared earlier.

"*Yoo-hoo*, lovebirds," Maddie interrupted. "I'd say go get a room, but I don't want to sleep on the couch tonight, so cut it out already, *hmmkay*?"

She had mellowed since returning from the parasailing adventure this afternoon. "I also have a gift; two gifts, actually. Except I'm not sure if you'll think they're presents or inconveniences."

"Oh, Maddie! No, you've given me so much already," Krista objected.

Her best friend had been her biggest benefactress since college. She was an only child with a French father who kept giving her material things to make up for his absence in her life. Clothes, shoes, books, meals, rides, and spa treatments were shared with Krista. All this and unconditional love and support were gifts she could never repay. Maddie was truly the sister of her heart.

"Krista, truthfully, you'll be the one doing me a favor if you agree to take these." She handed her two sets of keys. "For my apartment and my car. Now yours. Temporarily."

"What? Why?" Krista was stunned. *Maddie is leaving?* She took the keys automatically, not sure if she wanted to accept them.

"My company is assigning me to Singapore for three years starting in January as part of my promotion."

Blake whistled when he saw the keys. "We'll be neighbors, baby. And a Porsche 718 Boxster. Sweet ride. It's the red convertible, right? Didn't you just get that last week?"

Maddie nodded at Blake, but addressed Krista. "You don't look thrilled with my gifts, Krissy."

Both Blake and Maddie stared at her intently, waiting for her response. Her boyfriend appeared mystified by her lack of enthusiasm. Maddie looked nervously expectant.

Krista gave herself a mental smack in the head. She was being selfish, not wanting her friend to go. Maddie had been working to achieve this plum post for years. In her eyes, Krista could see the pride at the major accomplishment.

Her chair screeched loudly in her rush to stand up. Krista gave her friend a tight hug. "Oh, Mads. I *am* happy for you. A regional post? You've earned this. I'm just sad that we won't see each other regularly."

She put a hand over her chest. "And I'm overwhelmed with all these gifts! I'll take the fabulous apartment, but I'm going to have to decline the ten-million-pesos car." She stuck her tongue out at Blake when he groaned at the last bit. The playful gesture was met with a wink and a grin.

Krista's excitement over her friend's generous present grew. Living in Maddie's condominium rent-free for three years would enable her to save money for the future and create a tidy nest-egg for herself. Her one-bedroom apartment in Makati, while dinky, still took up twenty percent of her monthly income.

It would also allow her and Blake to keep their relationship private. They could be colleagues at work and lovers at home. No one at the office needed to know and harass them about their personal involvement. *Win-win.*

"That's okay," Maddie was saying as she sat back down. "I'll return it to the showroom; cancel my purchase."

"Why ever for?" Blake asked while holding out his hand to Krista. "Won't you lose a lot of money if you do that?"

Krista allowed herself to be pulled down to his lap. At this point, there was no use pretending they weren't intimately involved. A quick glance around reassured her that only a few of the hotel's guests remained in the restaurant, most of them foreigners.

"So that Krista can have parking space for her Toyota," Maddie replied. "The owner of the dealership is my client. It'll be fine. I only wanted the car because I like showing off my wealth, but I don't need it. Especially when I'll be gone anyway. How would people know it's mine if I'm not around to drive it?" She tossed her head in defiance.

"Mads, you're awfully hard on yourself."

"I'm just being honest—"

The blare of her phone's standard ringtone cut off her words. Some of Maddie's clients were internationally based, so she always kept her phone on for them. She held up a finger to excuse herself from the group and brought the phone to her ear.

"Madeleine Duvall speaking." Her eyes widened in surprise at the caller. She inclined her head to get Krista over to her side of the table.

"Farrah, hi! Yeah, I'm with your sister. You're right, she must have left her phone in our cottage. Sure, ring me back and I'll have her answer the vid call."

She clicked the off button and handed the phone to Krista, wagging her finger and grinning at her friend's chagrin. She moved to sit on the chair Aidan had vacated.

"Happy birthday, *Ate*!" A wave of affection swept over Krista as she was greeted by her spunky half-sister with a fond smile.

When seen side by side, their familial connection was undeniable, despite the differing skin tone and physical build. It showed in their shiny black hair, slanted brown eyes, the plump fullness of their lips, and the slope of their cheekbones.

"Thanks, Far. Sorry *ha*, I kept my phone off all day. Maddie arrived this morning," Krista threw a teasing glance at her friend, "and just talked, and talked, and talked. You know how she is." She placed the phone on its side, bracing it against a glass of water.

"It's okay. I figured you'd be out in the water or something. Hey, how do you like Boracay? I'm so *inggit*. Maybe once I'm off the nightshift I'll take some of my unused vacation leave and go there. Would you recommend that resort where you're staying?"

Krista eyed Blake who was unashamedly listening in to her conversation with her sister. "Perlas? It's … *uhm* … nice." Her tepid compliment had Blake clutching at his chest and wiping imaginary tears from his eyes as if brokenhearted. *That'll teach you to eavesdrop.*

"By nice, I mean here at Perlas you will be indulging in true relaxation of body and spirit, enjoying sumptuous feasts that tempt your taste buds at all hours of the day, beholding natural beauty so

175

unbelievably stunning that you'd think it's not real, and receiving service so warm and gracious that you wouldn't want to leave."

She heard Maddie's slow clap to her right, but she kept her gaze on Blake as she continued her praise. "If you look up images of paradise online, you'll find pictures of Perlas on the top of your search results."

He rose from the chair and walked towards her, his eyes ablaze with blue flames. Krista had forgotten she was talking to her sister. All her attention was focused on the man bent before her. He reached down and trailed his fingers over her hair, down her cheek, and across her lips. "You, my love, are a big tease," he whispered, then brought his mouth close to hers.

"*Ate, Nanay* and *Tatay* want to greet you. *Ay, lagot!* Caught in the act."

"*Anak*, happy—huh?" Her father's voice, loving then confused.

"Maria Krista Lopez! *Ano'ng ibig sabihin nito?* Who is this man, and what is he doing kissing you?" Her mother's shriek was sharp and accusatory.

"Shit *de la merde*!" Maddie cursed, succinctly expressing how Krista felt.

Stricken with guilt, Krista pushed Blake away and faced her parents. The tiny screen showed Blake's surprise, her *tatay*'s concern, her mom's anger, and her own red-faced shame. This was not how she wanted to make the introductions. It wasn't as if she and Blake were engaging in something illicit, something forbidden.

Krista knew it was the wrong thing to do, but as if of its own volition, her finger pressed the red button on the phone, abruptly ending the video call. Disrespectful and cowardly—that's what she was.

She kept her head down and felt the brush of air when Blake left her side. Without looking at him, she recognized his hurt.

"What's going on here?" Aidan broke the uncomfortable silence. He had returned only to see Krista's face buried in her hands, Maddie by her side, and his brother with his back to the two women, standing rigidly outside the gazebo, his jaw and fists clenched.

"That's what I want to know, too. It looked to me like my girlfriend doesn't want me to meet her family," Blake bit out.

The best friends gasped at the wrongful accusation. Krista got to her feet and placed her hand on her boyfriend's arm when she reached him. "No, Blake. It's not like that."

Just then, the phone rang again. It was either her father or her sister. She looked at Blake, at the phone, then back to Blake again. "Can we talk later so I can explain? Please?" She had to make amends to her parents first.

He nodded, but remained stiff and unyielding beneath her palm. Nevertheless, she gave him an apologetic squeeze. "I'm sorry." She ran back to the table to answer the phone.

Krista took a deep breath and pressed the answer button. As she guessed, her father was on the other end of the line. "*Tatay*, sorry *po* for turning the phone off. It was rude and discourteous. *I* was rude and discourteous."

"*Anak*, I understand. It was an awkward situation all around. Both you and your mother reacted poorly."

Krista teared up at her father's calm reaction and stalwart personality. Blood or not, Arsenio Lopez would always be her first love. "Thank you, *'Tay*. What about *Nanay*? Is she … is she angry with me? Does she not want to talk to me?"

"*Iha*, your mother loves you, never doubt that. You know how she feels about foreign men, especially Americans. The young man with you—he is American, would that be correct?" At her nod, he continued. "Marissa is afraid you will be left behind like she was. She never wants to see you get hurt."

"I do know that. But, it's an entirely different situation with me and Blake. We're different people from *Nanay* and John." She couldn't bring herself to call the other man her father, when the man on the phone was the one who had raised her and loved her, all her life.

"We've known each other for months now, not just one night. I know his last name, where his family lives. I've even met his brother," she said, defensive.

"I see. Is there any particular reason why you never told us about him? Your mother, she feels shocked—betrayed, when she saw you with a man we have not heard of. As if you are hiding him from us, keeping him a secret."

Krista pressed her fingertips to her forehead to rub away the beginnings of a headache. This was exactly what she'd wanted to avoid—explaining to other people how she and Blake came to be together.

They didn't have a traditional Filipino courtship. Their relationship was too modern, too Western in the eyes of her conservative parents. "Uhm, I wasn't really hiding him. We didn't actually become boyfriend and girlfriend until yesterday."

"Aaah, I see."

Clearly, he didn't, but she wasn't going to elaborate and invite more censure. The near-kiss they saw was the tamest of the intimacies she'd already shared with Blake. "*Tatay*, may I talk to *Nanay*?" She wanted to apologize. To explain her side.

"*Anak*, it might be for the best to allow her to cool down first. *Alam mo naman yun.* Let her get over her *tampo*. I am going to talk with her, relate what you told me."

He paused as if weighing his words. "How about you wait for me to call you when she is ready to listen to what you have to say?"

Krista understood. Yes, she knew Marissa Lopez well. Her mother was going to sulk. Her eldest daughter had disappointed her, disobeyed her. It didn't matter that she was already thirty years old and the eldest of her three children. Krista would always be a child in her mother's eyes.

There was nothing she could do but wait until her mom was willing to listen. "Okay *po*. I'll wait for your call. 'Night, *'Tay*."

Chapter Nineteen

Kasaysayan [ka-sai-sa-yan] n. – history.

Blake turned the porch lights on at the back of Krista's cottage and sat on the padded wooden glider. He had gone ahead to wait for her here after leaving orders for the staff to close the restaurant.

Aidan went back to the Maharlika Kubo, while Maddie waited for her best friend to finish her phone call with her father. He had also arranged a golf cart and driver to bring them back here when they were ready.

He now recognized his overreaction when he accused Krista of not wanting to introduce him to her family. She had beckoned to him with that tease about Perlas, knowing full well that he'd be visible to her sister when he came over. The tension only manifested when her mother had a violently negative reaction to their near-kiss.

In his conceit, it never occurred to him that her parents wouldn't approve of their relationship, wouldn't want him for their daughter. His experience was the exact opposite. Hopeful mamas had been introducing their daughters to him ever since he came to the country. His lips twisted in a cynical smile.

If he was to guess, his nationality was the cause of dismay. He would find out soon enough. He heard the women's voices through the open back door.

Blake got up and stood by the door to reveal his location to his girlfriend. Maddie saw him first. She gave him a warning glance and mouthed, "Be gentle," before giving her friend a hug and walking away to give them privacy.

Krista turned to face him, shoulders still hunched. Her eyes were bright with unshed tears, and her lips trembled. He rushed to her side and wrapped her in his arms. "I'm sorry, baby."

"I'm sorry, too. That wasn't the way I wanted you to meet my family, and my mom's reaction made me panic." She looked up at him, the tears she'd been holding back now flowing freely down her face.

"All my life, I've always done my best to make my parents proud of me. I never wanted to disappoint them, especially my mom. She gave me life when she could have easily just gotten rid of me … kept me when she could have … just given me away."

Voice breaking, she clutched at his shirt. "Blake, she wouldn't even talk to me … wouldn't let me explain …" Sobs wracked her frame, her knees buckled in her sorrow, her whole body sagged into his embrace.

Blake lifted her carefully and carried her to the sofa. He let her cry it out, offering his comfort by sitting quietly, rubbing her back. He knew the storm had passed when she lifted her head from his chest and attempted to pat down his damp shirt.

He cupped her cheek in his palm and with a gentle caress, wiped away the teardrops from her face. "You don't have to tell me anything now. I just hate seeing you so sad, knowing that I was partly responsible for it."

She shook her head vehemently. "No, Blake. It's not your fault. It's a long story, but you have a right to know. Especially if you really want a relationship with me beyond this week." She reached for a handful of tissues and delicately blew her nose.

It was Blake's turn to shake his head as she started to move off his lap. He kept his arm around her and brushed a soft kiss on her lips. "I'm here. I'll listen."

Krista gave him a grateful smile then took a deep breath. "As you might have already guessed, the man who raised me is not my biological father. Arsenio Lopez married my mother when she found herself pregnant after a one-night stand with an American airman.

Tatay had been in love with her since they met, you see. He still is. But, she was … she always preferred foreigners, which was why she went to work near the former Clark US Air Force Base in Pampanga, so far away from her own province in Quezon." She sniffed and continued. "My mother was nearly raped and my … John, the American … he saved her. He was her hero.

She fell in love with him, or at least she believed herself to be at the time. But, the next day he left … and never came back." She paused and gestured that she wanted to get a drink. Blake assisted her to her feet and watched as she walked to the kitchen to get water.

The damsel in distress and the knight in shining armor. It didn't only happen in books. He frowned in concentration and recalled what he learned during his briefing, before he came to the country.

The mid-to-late eighties was a chaotic time in the Philippines. The People Power Revolution toppled the strongman Ferdinand Marcos, then several attempted *coup d'états* failed to overthrow the administration of the country's first female president, and there was a constitutional change, among many momentous events.

John might have been called to the capital for a mission. It was also possible that he was deployed elsewhere. The Philippines wasn't the only country with a turbulent history during that time.

Krista returned and arranged herself back on Blake's lap. "So, this John—he never knew about you?"

"No. My mom said she waited until she was showing already, but she never saw him again at Clark. They didn't exchange numbers. She didn't even know his last name."

"I take it he wouldn't have suspected he got her pregnant because he used a condom." The blush on Krista's face amused him. He didn't want to think about his parents having sex, either.

"I assumed so. I didn't ask. I mean, that's not really something you—"

Blake gave her a squeeze. "I'm teasing, baby."

She smiled for the first time since the night's drama started and gave him a weak push on the shoulder. He took her hand and gave it a kiss. "So, your parents married because of you."

Krista nodded. "My dad said she had a tough time during the first trimester, looking for John and not finding him—neither of them had access to the base—then not being able to do her job as a cook well, because she couldn't take the smell and taste of food. She was throwing up all the time.

He was persistent in courting her, even though she told him she was bearing another man's child. After four months of futile waiting, she finally accepted his proposal and they moved to another town where nobody knew them."

Even if John had been re-assigned to the Philippines before the base closed, he wouldn't have found Krista's mom again. "Were things difficult when you were younger?" Being born from a mixed union was more accepted now, but three decades ago there might still have been a lot of stigma.

"In the beginning, no. When I was little, I looked enough like my mother—it didn't matter that I was lighter-skinned than my siblings. *Nanay* has Spanish blood, and she always kept me indoors and dressed me in long-sleeved clothes. But, I grew and grew, taller than my classmates and taller than my parents. When we'd go out as a family I'd stand out, and not in a good way."

It became obvious that she wasn't her Filipino father's child. Blake's heart went out to the young Krista, whose only fault was to be born. He enfolded her in a tight hug. "Sweetheart, I'm so sorry for your hurt."

She returned his embrace and they were silent for a while.

"I was subjected to names like 'changeling,' 'albino,' 'child out of wedlock,' and 'mongrel.' Scholastically, I was at the top of the class, and I was physically bigger than anybody else, so the taunts just rolled off my back. Sticks and stones and all that.

My adoptive father's position also helped. He taught math at the same school the three of us attended. All students had to go through his class so they could graduate. He declared on the first day of class that insults against me were insults against him." Love and pride in the man who raised her rang clearly in her words.

"Your dad sounds like a good man," he observed.

"The very best." She nodded emphatically. "But my mom, it was she who suffered the brunt of the censure." Her tone turned serious, her voice started to break again. "There was a whole period of time when she was estranged from her parents, when the rumormongers were actively maligning her reputation. Lies were being spread about her—she was a prostitute in Angeles City, she cheated on my father with an American GI, etcetera.

She couldn't keep a job, she became reclusive—wouldn't even go to church." Tears started to fall again from her eyes. She immediately brushed them away. "There were times that she looked at me as if she regretted keeping me; that she hated me for causing all her troubles.

Then, she'd smother me with attention. She was overprotective in my teens; wouldn't let me do anything or go anywhere not connected with school." Krista grimaced at the memory. "And she fed me. God, how she fed me. We didn't have a lot of money, but we never starved because my mother knew how to grow herbs and vegetables, how to raise chickens and pigs in the little space we had. You know how Filipinos are known to eat six times a day?"

It was a rhetorical question, but he answered anyway. "Yes. Breakfast, morning snack, lunch, afternoon snack, dinner, and midnight snack," he rattled off. He always marveled at how his employees could pack away so much, yet stay so slim.

"Exactly. All I did throughout high school was study and eat. Without exercise, except for PE in school, I ballooned to over 200 pounds." She wiggled on his lap. "Had we met then, we wouldn't have been able to do this. You wouldn't have been able to take my weight. I'd have flattened you," she stated matter-of-factly.

Krista was right. He was skin and bones in middle school. Bouncing his knees, he told her, "Well, you're in perfect health now, so I've no complaints. I wasn't the healthiest of teenagers, either. I was a late bloomer." She raised her eyebrow, disbelief written on her face.

"It's true. I was pimply and scrawny. I'll show you some pictures someday." He'd introduce Krista to his parents. For sure, his mother would be psyched to bring out the old albums.

She rubbed his cheek with hers, then rested her head against his neck. "I'd love to see them." Wistful longing tinged her voice. "Someday."

Blake kept quiet. He just sat there nuzzling her hair, waiting for her to continue her story.

"My mother had seriously conflicting feelings about my birth father. She was both angry at him and defensive of him. One day she'd tell me he was honorable, and had he known about me, he would have done the right thing.

At other times she'd rail at him—at all white men. She would tell me, '*Anak*, promise me you will not fall in love with a foreigner, particularly an American. They will only break your heart. Find a nice Filipino man like your *tatay*.' I would just nod and say yes. What else was I supposed to say?"

Blake winced at the confirmation of the rough road he would need to take, to find favor with her mother. There it was—why she'd tried to keep her distance, despite their mutual attraction. The reason she couldn't say "I love you" back. To fulfill her Turning-Thirty Vow by being with him, she had broken another.

"When I decided to apply at the universities in Manila and Quezon City, my mom and I had a huge row. She didn't want me at the big city. She didn't want me out of her sight." Krista heaved a deep sigh.

"Thankfully, my dad was on my side. As an educator, he recognized that the provincial colleges couldn't provide the same opportunities a UP or Ateneo degree would give me. My mom had no choice but to let me go."

Blake knew the rest of the story. She met Maddie and the rest of her squad, *M'amie*, at the University of the Philippines. She worked as a student and research assistant to earn some extra money while completing a five-year course in four. With high honors to boot.

He figured the university was where she lost weight, gained confidence, and found her own identity. Away from the controlling influence of her parent. Away from the guilt and blind obedience required of her because of her mother's history.

What does it mean for us moving forward? He knew it wasn't fair to ask Krista now, when she was still so emotional, but he couldn't help himself. He needed a plan of action. If there was a problem, he wanted it solved. "What do we do now?"

She leaned back to look at him, a frown marring her beautiful face. "I … I don't think we can do anything now. While we're here in Boracay, I mean. My mom didn't want to talk to me. I have to wait until she calms down." She rubbed her forehead. "I want them to meet you; get to know you. I want them to realize that you're different. You're not John."

"No, I'm not." He could hear a "but" coming.

"But," Krista gave a helpless shrug, "not yet. My mom could take a long time to get over her sulk. She didn't speak to me for months when I started college; didn't even go with my dad and siblings when I moved to my dorm." She stroked his arm in a plea for understanding. "Is it okay if we table the meeting until she's more open to giving you a chance?"

Blake heard the exhaustion in her voice, so he didn't argue. She was also right—they still had three days in the island. Less than that. It was Thursday already. But he couldn't let her go to sleep feeling sad. "You know, there's a silver lining in all this."

"What's that?" She hid a yawn behind her hand.

"Your mom would have had a heart attack if it was Aidan she saw you kissing."

Her eyes widened, and her mouth formed a big "O." "Blake!" She flicked her hand on his shoulder but let out a reluctant giggle.

"Think about it. White guy, close-cropped hair, shoulders square. She might not have seen the stick up his well-disciplined ass, but everything about my brother screams military. There's John 2.0, right there." He grinned when Krista's giggle turned into full-blown laughter, until tears ran down her cheeks again. These tears he liked. It made him happy that he caused them.

With a hiccup, she captured his face between her hands and gazed at him tenderly. "Oh Blake, you're wonderful. Thank you. I—"

"Could you two turn it down? Trying to sleep here." Maddie demanded as she came out of the bedroom. Her face was wreathed in smiles, relieved her friend's sadness had passed.

Blake groaned and threw his head back against the couch. The woman had the worst timing in the world.

Krista gave him an apologetic smile and turned to her best friend. "Blake just said I'm lucky my mom saw him instead of Aidan. She would have died on the spot." She left her perch on his lap to stand beside her friend.

Maddie snorted. "Good one, Blake. Now, you go kissy-kissy and let us go to bed. I need my beauty sleep, even if you two don't." With that pronouncement, she marched back to the bedroom.

"Your friend is a menace," he said without real resentment. He got to his feet and reached for Krista, bestowing a soft kiss on her lips. "Good night, baby. I love you." He didn't wait for her response; he left with a light heart.

THURSDAY

Chapter Twenty

Salamat [sa-la-mat] n. – thanks.

Krista watched Aidan wipe the oil and grime off his hands with a rag; he'd just finished checking the small plane for its flight readiness. Earlier, she saw him show his credentials to the resort pilots and heard him ask respectfully if he could help them do the pre-flight inspection.

Behind her, Maddie and Blake were consulting on a PR campaign. While the two were engrossed in the papers they had spread out on the coffee table in the small departure lounge at Perlas' mini-air strip, Krista decided to talk to Aidan.

They still had thirty minutes before Maddie and Aidan departed for Makati, and Krista wanted to take advantage of the lull to learn something more about Blake. She was almost sure of her feelings for him—she'd nearly declared it last night—but any little bit of information might help get her to one-hundred-percent certainty.

Krista sat by the door so Aidan would see her right away when he came in from the hangar.

"Is everything all right?" she asked as he approached. *How could the pilots say no to this guy?* He was not only a foot taller than them, his rank showed in the commanding way he carried himself. He again wore a crisp gray dress shirt, freshly pressed blue slacks, and shiny black shoes. Not the usual island uniform, that, except for the Ray-Bans. If her biological father looked like Aidan when her mother met him, it was no wonder her mom gave in to lust-at-first-sight.

Frankly, Aidan intimidated her. He resembled Blake, but he was harder and more guarded than her boyfriend. Although they shared the same birthday, Krista wasn't sure if she could ever feel comfortable with Aidan. Maybe familiarity would cure that. At the moment though, she felt anxious. He had waved away her apology this morning—Blake must have shared with him some of her explanation—but she still felt as if he was judging her and finding her lacking.

Aidan sat beside her and nodded. "All good. They're competent pilots. The plane is fairly new and well-maintained." He took off his sunglasses and looked at her with his piercing blue-gray eyes. "But, that wasn't why you want to talk to me right now. You'd like to get the dirt on Blake, right?"

Krista flushed. "Not the dirt, exactly. Anything that will help me understand him better would be welcome. Right now, I only know of his professional accomplishments and what he's shown me these past few days. You could say that since we are in a courtship stage, he's been putting his best foot forward, as the cliché goes." She sighed and looked at Aidan. "After last night, I feel at a disadvantage; I've shown my flaws, and yet he remains almost perfect."

Aidan chuckled. "Trust me, he's far from perfect. He's a big mama's boy, he hates being laughed at, he is risk averse, and he can be materialistic. You may have noticed he likes to manage things and organize people. That comes from being a middle child." He paused and considered her briefly. "Do you have siblings?"

"Yeah. I'm the eldest of three. My sister, Farrah, is next, then Alex." *How is this important?*

"So, we have that in common as well as sharing the same birthday." He smiled at her, his attitude towards her seeming to thaw considerably. "Blake was the baby of the family very briefly before he was followed by Craig, so he was never the one pampered. You might say he was ignored a lot, especially when Darcy came along. Being autocratic is his way of making sure he gets noticed and recognized."

"I see. That explains a lot. Thank you. What do you mean by him being risk averse?" She got that bit about the materialistic trait already. She noticed that Blake liked to accumulate material wealth. The Louboutins he gave her still made her wince. She could buy a hundred pairs of locally-made shoes for the same price.

"He's often skeptical about new opportunities," Aidan replied. "He is exceedingly cautious. He seeks stability rather than conquering new challenges. You know he's been living here in the Philippines for five years. He's also been with the same company since he got his MBA."

That made sense. She, herself, had worked for three companies already within nine years. Blake only worked for one in eleven years. "But what about ..."

"… the resort?" Aidan finished for her. "You can bet the other partners took a long time to woo him, quite possibly years. And, he was the last one to agree. He'd have already researched, taken all the facts into account, and received guarantees that he would be in control before he made the decision."

Krista bowed her head. This was the difficult part. "What about relationships?"

"You're his first real one." The statement was stark. She lifted her head in disbelief.

"That can't be. Isn't he thirty-three? He must have had girlfriends before." *How could that be? Blake must be considered quite the catch, even in the US, with his good looks and deep pockets.*

Aidan shook his head. "No one he introduced to the family. He's always been shy, especially around girls. He was gangly and nerdy in high school. It took a while for him to grow out of it." His gaze hardened briefly, as if a memory had flashed through his mind. "Isn't he your first relationship, too?"

"Yes. He's my first boyfriend." *Hopefully the last.*

"Like with this resort, Blake must have weighed the pros and cons before he resolved to pursue you and decided you're worth any obstacles that would come your way. Be careful with his heart, Krista. My brother waited a long time before he got into a committed relationship. I would hate to see him hurt." There was a clear warning in Aidan's voice.

Scorpios were notorious for their vengeful nature. She wouldn't want to be on the receiving end of this man's retribution.

"I will," she promised. She lifted her chin and looked Aidan in the eye. "As long as he doesn't break my heart, I will be careful with his."

He inclined his head in acknowledgment. They understood one another.

Krista glanced at the table where Maddie and Blake seemed to be finishing their business meeting. She turned back to Aidan and blurted out, "One more thing, Aidan."

A raised eyebrow was her prompt to continue. She really wanted to ask, *Can you help me find my father?* but opted for, "Please look after Maddie in Singapore. She may act tough, but she needs someone to take care of her. Will you do that … for Blake … and me?"

He hesitated for just a beat. "I will look after Madeleine as much as she will allow me to." It was a vow from a man who recognized his equal.

Krista impulsively leaned over and gave Aidan a hug. "Thank you."

To her shock, he said the ritual reply in Filipino. "*Walang anuman.*"

She reared back, gaping at him. He was smiling. "*Tita* Belen is not only Blake's. She is an honorary aunt to all of the Ryan kids."

"Oops. I forgot. Sorry!" She flushed in embarrassment, then broke into giggles when he spoke in the native language again. "*Walang problema.*"

Yep, there's no problem, indeed.

***

195

Blake was happy to see his brother and his girlfriend getting along so well. He worried last night that Aidan would have a negative impression of Krista after the drama with her parents. An impression he caused with his unfounded accusation.

This morning, he'd briefly explained her mother's opposition to Krista's relationship with an American. It crossed his mind to ask for Aidan's help to find her birth father, but he had to discuss it with his girlfriend first.

Seeing them laugh together pleased him. They were more than likely talking about him; he didn't mind being their topic of conversation if it helped Krista feel surer about him.

"Krista loves you, you know," Maddie said, breaking his thoughts. She was also observing her friend and his brother.

"I do know. I'm not jealous of that. I trust them both," he assured Maddie. Blake knew where his brother's interests lay—on the woman in front of him, not on Krista.

"No. I didn't imply that. I meant she must not have told you yet." Maddie looked at him as if seeking confirmation. "She wouldn't have slept with you if she wasn't already in love with you."

You butted in before she could tell me. "She hasn't yet, but I don't mind. I feel her love every time she smiles at me and with the way she responds to my touch. I can wait until Krista is ready to tell me." He was a patient man, but he had a feeling he didn't have long to wait anyway.

196

"Krista doesn't say it often. Her family isn't overly affectionate; she didn't grow up hearing it said to her. Most Filipinos don't, except in movies or books," Maddie explained. "She has only told me she loves me a couple of times, and we've been friends for fourteen years." She sighed. "What I'm trying to say in a long-winded way is that when she tells you she loves you—I say when, not if—it means she's all in. You are it for her. So, do *not* break her heart, or I'll make you regret you ever came to the Philippines." Maddie shook her fists at him.

Blake burst out laughing. These two were so delightful. No wonder he and his brother were attracted to these women. The Ryan brothers had to be secret masochists, because Krista and Maddie were both hell on wheels. But so worth it.

He stood and held his right hand over his heart, swearing sincerely, "I promise." After a beat, he said, "Now come on. I think Aidan is finished spilling all my secrets to your best friend."

Striding to where the two were seated, he said loudly, "Bro, find your own woman. This one is mine."

He leaned down and pulled Krista to her feet to kiss her lightly on the lips. Only the four of them were in the room, so he had no qualms about showing affection. Krista seemed to be getting comfortable with their intimacy; she wrapped her arms around his waist and lay her head on his shoulder.

She tapped his chest and said, "Blake, don't be rude. Aidan and I were just talking. He didn't tell me anything incriminating about you, but we exchanged e-mail addresses. If you're mean to me, I'll download the baby pictures he's going to send me and show them to everyone in the office." He knew she was joking. He saw her wink at Aidan.

Amused, he said, "I don't care. I was cute in diapers. Craig was the ugly one—he looked like a miniature Michelin Man." His brother guffawed, and he laughed too. They really needed to get together soon. He missed his family.

Krista disentangled herself from him and muttered, "*Hambog*," before thumping him on the chest again. After calling him a braggart, his girlfriend moved away to talk to Maddie.

Blake stepped closer to his brother. "When do you go back to Singapore?"

"I'm not sure yet. I have a meeting at the US Embassy all day tomorrow, then I'll be free after that. My plans are flexible," Aidan replied while looking at Maddie. "I can return any time before Monday morning."

If Blake had to guess, Aidan would show up for a visit at his apartment in Bonifacio Global City sometime Saturday or Sunday afternoon, or whenever Maddie and Aidan came up for air.

He smiled at his brother knowingly. "If you have a few minutes to spare before you go, just give me a ring or knock on my door. It's just a floor above hers." Blake chuckled when his brother glowered at him.

"What's so funny?" Krista asked him as she and Maddie joined them to say their farewells. The plane was ready for boarding.

"I'll tell you later." He winked at Krista and gave Maddie a brotherly hug. "Take it easy on Aidan. He's not used to being on the receiving end of a whip," he whispered. He chuckled again when she reddened and bared her teeth at him.

She turned to Krista and complained, "I hate your boyfriend. He thinks he's so clever."

Krista just laughed and hugged Maddie. "That's because he is. Have a safe flight. See you in Makati."

Krista stepped back and gripped Blake's outstretched hand as they watched Aidan and Maddie pretend to keep a distance between them that fooled no one at all.

Chapter Twenty-One

Tulog [too-lawg] n. – sleep.

"Alone at last," Blake said into Krista's hair. They were riding the golf cart back to the cottages. "What would you like to do today?" It was only eleven in the morning, but he could see that his woman's energy was flagging.

She might just want to be lazy today and not engage in anything more strenuous than talk, eat, and sleep. Although the mood was light during their late breakfast, he saw Krista hide a yawn behind her hand every so often. The best friends might have talked after he left, even though Maddie shooed him out on the pretext of going to bed.

As he guessed, she said, "At some point I would like to check out the boutiques, but can we just take it easy today? Lounge by the whirlpool? Eat a late lunch? Yesterday was great but long and incredibly eventful." She smiled at him wearily.

"Have I thanked you yet for organizing everything for Aidan's and my birthday? I had so much fun, except for the last five minutes of dinner, of course." Her face contorted with regret at the memory of the drama.

"You have thanked me with every smile on your face, with every sparkle in your eyes, and with every laugh that has passed your lips. Your enjoyment is all the gratitude I need, and you've given me that already, so you're very welcome." He tightened his arms around her and pressed a kiss on her forehead. "Where do you want to relax? My *kubo* or yours?"

She leaned away and looked up at him. "I've already checked out of my cottage. I asked housekeeping to move my things to yours." She peered at him from beneath her lashes. "I hope that's all right. I should have asked you first." She looked prepared for rejection. "I'm sorry."

Joy leapt in his chest, and a huge smile covered his face. "No, don't be sorry. I should have thought of it myself. I just didn't want to rush you more than I already have." He took her back in his embrace.

Her initiatives in the forward progress of their relationship delighted him—Monday's strip poker, and this move to be with him for the next fifty-plus hours while they were still in Boracay.

They had reached his *kubo*—correction, their *kubo*—and he assisted Krista down from the vehicle. Nodding his thanks to the driver, he opened the door to his cottage and lifted Krista in his arms. She yawned again.

"Come on, baby. Off to bed with you. Let's tuck you in for a nap." He laid her gently on the bed. "Let me take off your bra so you'll feel more comfortable."

She kicked off her sandals and got under the blankets, muttering drowsily, "No need. Not wearing a bra. Friends didn't pack any in suitcase." She removed her ponytail and shook out her hair to let it fan around her head on the pillow. "Night, hon."

MAIDA MALBY

She murmured something else, but he didn't catch it. *Did she say, "I love you," or "I owe you"?* He laughed softly at himself. For someone who claimed to be patient, he was trying to hasten this process of hearing her say the magic words to him. He thought she'd been about to tell him last night after she talked about her mother. She started to say "I," but Maddie interrupted. That wasn't the right time—not when she was coming from an emotional roller coaster.

He also didn't want her to tell him when she was half-asleep, like a few moments ago. What made him happy was that it was already inside her heart. When the perfect time came, the words would be out of her lips with no hesitation or conditions.

In the meantime, he would set up their lunch for two pm and confirm Krista's check-out with Perlas' management. He'd make sure they didn't charge Maddie's credit card for Friday and Saturday nights. Then, he would join his woman for a nap.

***

Krista stretched and was momentarily startled when her hands grazed a warm body beside her on the bed. *Blake.* She smiled and curled up on her side to stare adoringly at his sleeping form. This was only the third time they'd slept together, but it was starting to become a habit she didn't want to break.

It all started Monday night when she seduced him into taking her virginity. Krista flushed at how brazen she was, how forward. He woke her up the next day super sweetly and treated her to the best birthday celebration a woman could ever have.

Yesterday morning started so great with his wake-up kiss that was cut short by the arrival of Maddie and Aidan. With Maddie there, she had no choice but to sleep without him for one night. She'd missed him and couldn't wait to see him again this morning

While Maddie was packing, Krista realized it made no sense to keep two cottages; she and Blake were together all the time anyway. She started to pack her own things, and checked out of her *kubo* before meeting Blake and Aidan at the air strip.

He was stunned, happily so, when she'd told him she planned to move to his cottage for the rest of their stay at Perlas. After a slight moment of panic that he might not like her assertiveness, she was gratified by his authentically eager response.

She thought it was time to show him she was ready to take an equal role in their relationship. Maybe not in terms of material gifts, but she could reciprocate by giving him something of value that money couldn't buy—her wholehearted love.

I will give him the words. Oh yes, I will tell him I love him, and I know exactly how to do it. Not when I'm crying and laughing like an insane person. Not when I'm about to fall asleep. No, when I tell him, we will both be aware, and he will know how significant the words are to me. For now, I will demonstrate my love in action and deeds. With my mouth, hands, and body.

A seductive smile came over Krista's face as she pulled the bedsheets slowly down his body. As expected, Blake wore only his boxer briefs to bed. *He is so beautiful.*

At first, she'd wondered how a desk rider like him could be so fit and muscular. But she had seen his dedication to health and fitness these past few days and doubted no more. She removed her clothes quickly and returned to his side.

Trailing her fingertips on his chest, she paid close attention to his nipples, which were hardening with her every touch. She ruffled the hair that arrowed down to his groin, smiling when she saw Blake's body start to wake with her ministrations.

Lightly tracing his shape through the silk of his underwear, she felt it continue to harden beneath her fingers. When she reached to release his erection from its confines, a hand snaked out to grab hers, stopping Krista from her explorations. His half-lidded gaze burned with blue fire.

"Dare," Krista whispered, to remind him of their first night together. He slowly removed the hand that imprisoned hers and put it behind his head, giving her complete access to his body. She moved down the bed to sit on her haunches by his legs.

Keeping her eyes locked on his, she hooked her fingers into the waistband of his boxer briefs and pulled them off, leaving him gloriously naked. His nostrils flared at the brush of her fingers along the insides of his thighs. She abruptly stopped her exploration of his body when he started to close his eyes.

"Eyes on me, honey," Krista commanded. So, this was why he kept saying that to her during their lovemaking. The power of seeing his reaction to her touch coursed through her, making her achy and slick, and ready to accept him into her body. But she had to taste him first. She had never done it, yet she was sure he would appreciate her innocent attempts to bring him sexual gratification.

She finally brought her hands together to close her fingers on his erection, and he groaned in response. Still watching him, she leaned down to take him into her mouth. *Hmm, hard but soft, too, and musky. Supremely male.* She licked beneath the head. making his body jerk on the bed. *Utterly delectable.*

"Krista, baby, if you don't stop that. I'll come in your mouth."

That's not much of a threat, big guy, she thought. *That's exactly what I want you to do.* She winked at him and instead of letting him go, Krista tightened her grip on his arousal and continued with the wet strokes of her tongue on his hard flesh.

She licked up and down his erection, over the head, teasing it with the tip of her tongue while her hands continued to fondle him. Breathing through her nose, Krista slid her lips further down his hardness, taking more of him, taking him deeper. She didn't stop until he gave in to the pleasure and released into her loving mouth.

Chapter Twenty-Two

Chismis [cheese-miss] n. – gossip.

Blake gazed affectionately at Krista as she talked to the sales assistant in the boutique. She was buying souvenirs for her family to make up for not spending her thirtieth birthday with them. Even though things were still unsettled between her and her mother, she wanted to show them her love and appreciation.

She was also buying presents for her group of friends to thank them for paying for this holiday at Perlas.

Blake wanted to offer to pay for the thank-you gifts because it wasn't just Krista who had benefited from their largesse—he had, too. If not for them, he and Krista wouldn't have had this week to get together and fall in love. But, he knew his proud girlfriend wouldn't like that.

His woman was so fiercely independent, and he respected that about her.

He would just make sure her friends received a generous discount at Perlas whenever they chose to vacation in Boracay. He'd tell Maddie that he owed them all for this golden opportunity to get close to Krista.

His loins tightened when he realized how close they had become, especially her generous loving this afternoon when he woke up from his nap.

He had never seen her as sensual as when she made love to his body.

He'd wanted to return the favor, but her stomach had growled with hunger and she broke into peals of laughter at the indelicate sound. They had dressed quickly and ordered whatever was fastest at the restaurant.

Tonight, he'd make sure no inch of her silky, smooth skin was neglected. He would kiss her until she was mindless with the same pleasure she gave him today, and every time they made love.

"All done?" he asked as Krista approached carrying several *bayong* bags containing her purchases. The bags, made from woven strips of dried palm leaves, were especially handmade for the resort by the survivors of Super Typhoon Yolanda from Panay Island.

Blake personally supported several charities that benefited victims of the Philippines' many natural disasters, preferring those which provided livelihood and sustainable income rather than mere temporary aid.

"Yes. I can't get over how great the selections are here. This boutique can easily compete with any of those high-end stores in Greenbelt," Krista replied enthusiastically.

Blake drew her close and caught her lips in a kiss, charmed by her total enjoyment of her shopping experience at Perlas' *Sari-Sari* store.

"Where to now?" Blake asked, helping Krista with some of her *bayong* bags.

"Dinner!" she announced, her eyes bright with impish delight.

"Shopping makes you ravenous, huh?" he joked. He wasn't in the slightest bit hungry after their late lunch, but he could eat something light.

"Starved," Krista exclaimed, crossing her eyes and comically lolling out her tongue.

Blake chuckled at her antics. "Come on then, let's feed you before you expire from weariness and hunger."

They had no sooner sat down at the restaurant than Blake's phone rang. He frowned when he saw that it was his direct line at the Makati office.

Most of the staff, including his secretary, went back to work today after the long All Saints' Day break. *What couldn't wait until Monday?*

"Miss Malou, how was your vacation?" At Krista's questioning look, he just shrugged and mouthed, "*I don't know.*"

"It was fine, Blake." His secretary was one of the few people in the office he allowed to address him informally—everybody else called him Mr. Ryan.

"*Yours* is the reason I'm calling. I overheard a couple of girls from the marketing department gossiping about you and Krista Lopez. They claim to have seen the two of you kissing at D'Mall. I didn't confront them, as I didn't know if it was true. Be careful, Blake. This rumor will probably spread around the whole office tomorrow. Do you want me to say anything?"

He scowled and balled his fist on the table. *Fuck. I knew this was coming. Damn it.* He glanced at Krista, who was waving away the waiter and looking at him anxiously.

His voice was hard when he responded. He didn't care if his secretary knew he was pissed off. "Miss Malou, I'd appreciate it if you can remind the staff my personal life is no one's business but my own. I will say the same about Ms. Lopez's and everybody else's lives.

Please also check with HR regarding office policy on rumormongering, and e-mail it to me as soon as you find out. I'll deal with it when I return on Monday. Thank you for bringing this to my attention right away." *Fucking busybodies.*

"They know about us? Everybody at the office knows?" Krista was close to tears, her voice trembling with panic.

He frowned at her reaction. *So what if everyone found out? Didn't you agree to be my girlfriend? Why am I the only one willing to take on all the risks here?* "Not yet, but by tomorrow they all will."

Suddenly irritated with Krista and her unwillingness to fully commit to him, Blake prepared to go. He tucked his phone into his shorts' pocket and collected her shopping bags.

"Do you mind if we just have some food delivered to the cottage? I don't feel like being out in public right now."

"I don't mind," said Krista, as subdued as he felt.

Uneasy silence accompanied their ride back to their cottage. Blake put down her bags and moved to the window to look out at the garden. For a change,

209

the view wasn't soothing to him. First it was her mom, now this.

When Krista stepped close beside him, he asked, "What is so shameful about being with me?"

She looked up at him, her expression defensive. "You're misinterpreting my reaction, Blake. I am proud to be with you. Who wouldn't be?" Her chin jutted out.

"I panicked, okay? My mind went straight to worst-case scenario—that I'll lose my job. Or, even if I don't, I won't have any chance for a raise or a promotion because people will question it."

She reached for his hands. Pressing them in a plea for understanding, she said, "I'm sorry I didn't immediately think about us. Between my mom's disapproval and my fears, I'm a mess. I'm still reeling from the breakneck speed our relationship has been going so far. But I'm trying to keep up. I really am."

That mollified him somewhat. "I know. As you heard, I didn't confirm the gossip Miss Malou overheard. But I didn't deny it, either. If you're still uncomfortable about people knowing about us, we don't have to make any announcements on Monday. We can keep our distance at work. If we don't feed the fire, it will die down eventually."

He saw relief cross Krista's features at his suggestion, and he didn't like it. *Not one bit.*

Although he shared her distaste for being in the spotlight, he would have liked to see her fight for them instead of preferring to hide. *Whatever happened to* carpe diem?

He softened his tone, but made sure she realized that his patience had an expiration date.

"Krista, at some point you'll have to make a decision about your feelings for me. There will come a time when I'll think of your reluctance to make a full commitment as rejection. Be careful it doesn't come to that. I don't much care for unrequited love."

He let go of her hands gently. "Go on and order dinner for yourself. I'm going for a walk. I didn't have my daily swim, and I need the exercise."

He kissed her on her forehead and stepped out of the cottage, his earlier promise of making love to her all night long forgotten in his need to brood.

FRIDAY

Chapter Twenty-Three

Tatu [ta-too] n. – tattoo.

Krista experienced a sense of *déjà vu*. She was strolling on the beach again while Blake swam in the sea. Had it only been a week since she decided to make significant changes in herself? In her life? It had only been seven days since she decided to fulfill her Turning-Thirty Vow, but it seemed light-years away. She was a hugely different woman now from the Krista who had arrived in Boracay.

She vaguely remembered the prim, repressed woman who was annoyed with her friends for replacing her conservative clothes with figure-hugging outfits. *Who knew I'd be comfortable parading around half-naked in tiny bikinis and flimsy sarongs?* Not the Krista Lopez who left her small apartment at dawn on Saturday morning.

Over the next few months, she would make significant changes to her office clothes. They wouldn't be as revealing as her Boracay clothes, but neither would they be as shapeless as her old ones. She'd look for fashionable outfits that fit well and flattered her curves. Krista was sure her *barkada* would be only too willing to assist her with the making-over of her wardrobe.

Krista smiled in anticipation of her future shopping sprees. She'd never realized how enjoyable they could be until this week, especially yesterday. No wonder Blake loved shopping for gifts for her and his brother on their birthday. It was so much fun.

Blake. Aaah, Mr. Blake Ryan, Chief Executive Officer. The Hunk of Global City. My first kiss, first touch, first lover. My first love. Who'd have thought the man she shouted at on Saturday could be the one who turned virginal Krista into a sensual woman in full bloom? The heroines in her romance novels had nothing on her now.

Her smile dropped and her brows furrowed as she recalled last night's misunderstanding. Stepping into the shade of a coconut tree, she considered the most recent discord in their fledgling relationship.

Essentially, he had issued an ultimatum. It was totally unnecessary—she was ready to tell him she loved him—but he left before she could say anything. He must have seen her relief at his statement that they didn't have to make their personal connection known right away, and thought she was still harboring doubts.

In her defense, they hadn't yet talked about how they would deal with the fact that they worked in the same company. There hadn't been time. She had hoped maybe they could ease into the revelation at the office instead of making a grand announcement upon their return from Boracay. But yesterday's rumors forced their hand into making decisions right away.

Not that they agreed. Blake's managing personality came to the forefront once again. That was classic Mr. High-And-Mighty Ryan right there, when he dictated what they would do on Monday rather than wait until they came up with a plan together.

How could he still doubt my love for him? She broke her promise to her mother that she wouldn't fall for a foreigner. Her first try, and look what she got. An American with a brother who was in the Air Force. *Great job, vow-breaker.*

Krista huffed and leaned her head back against the tree. She understood where he was coming from. Nobody could change their personality in mere days. Aidan had said Blake was risk averse, but he laid himself bare by being open about his love for her. That she held back must have made him feel he wasn't in control—something he wasn't used to experiencing.

Her heart clenched in regret at her insensitivity. *I didn't realize how much power I have.* She and Maddie had talked about protecting her heart because Blake had the potential to break it. But they didn't consider the possibility that she had the power to break his. Aidan did. He warned her yesterday. Krista sighed. They both still had a lot to learn about navigating this relationship.

It must have been after midnight when he came back last night. She woke up in the middle of the night to find his arms around her. That brought a smile to her face, and she went back to sleep thinking they were all right. When they got up, they acted like yesterday's disagreement hadn't happened. There was no coolness, but there wasn't real warmth, either. They seemed to be in limbo; at a stalemate.

Krista slapped her hand on her forehead as the realization hit her. "Because it's your turn, dummy!" Like they said in sports, the ball was in her court. *Blake is still waiting for me to say I love him!* She'd already told him with her body and her actions. She'd said it in her head a thousand times. But she had never spoken the words out loud.

"I love you, Blake," Krista whispered, testing it out.

"I love you, Blake." Louder this time.

"I love you, Blake!" She yelled to the cloudless blue sky.

"I LOVE YOU, BLAKE RYAN!" Krista shouted to the dazzlingly aquamarine waters.

The sheer joy of finally letting it all out made her laugh out loud. She'd started the week seeking something extraordinary to do for her thirtieth birthday and had found a singular gift beyond her wildest dreams.

Krista was experiencing the most life-changing event anyone could ever go through—loving someone special, and having The One love her in return. She looked up to the sky one last time. "This is for you, Sheila."

Elated, Krista ran to the cottage to change her clothes. She arrived just in time to hear her cellphone ringing. She had forgotten it again. Shaking her head at her negligence, she reached for it, only to be brought up short by the caller ID. Their landline in Lucena—her parents' home in Quezon.

"*Tatay?*" Her heart was racing.

"Krista … *Anak.*" The feminine voice was thick with emotion.

"*Nanay.*" Krista could only croak her mother's name. "I'm sorry. I'm so very sorry I broke my promise to you. *Pero, mahal ko po si* Blake. And he loves me, too."

"I'm sorry, also. I should not have asked you to make that vow. You have a right to fall in love with whomever you feel is worthy of you." Regret tinged every word. "Your *tatay* scolded me, you know. He told me everything you said. Reminded me that you're already thirty, and you're very smart." Her mother was quiet for a beat. "This Blake, he is your boss?"

"*Opo.*"

"And you've met his family?"

"His brother Aidan came to visit him here in Boracay. We have the same birthday."

She went silent again. Krista thought she'd hung up the phone.

"Come to Lucena. You and Blake, come and see us. We'd like to meet your young man."

Krista couldn't help it. She burst into tears. "*Salamat po.* Thank you. We'll be there tomorrow. I love you, *Nanay.* You and *Tatay.* I love you so much."

"*Mahal din kita,* Krista. See you tomorrow."

Yes! Yes! Yes! Krista danced and jumped around the cottage as if she'd just knocked out an opponent in boxing. *I have to tell Blake.* She stopped. *No, I'll tell him everything tonight. After I say the words.*

She'd do more than say them. She would make a big statement. After tonight, there should be no question in Blake's mind of her sincerity and commitment. She had to get that tattoo done. It was time to declare her new motto. It was time to proclaim her love to the whole world. Carpe diem! *Seize the day, Krista!*

***

She is *doing it.* Blake was stunned when he arrived at the tattoo studio in D'Mall. Krista sat astride a chair with her front against its back, her chosen motto "*Carpe Diem*" being marked on her back. He followed her after seeing her note at the kubo, telling him where she had gone.

Blake hadn't been one hundred percent sure she would go through with it. Sunday was the first and last time they'd talked of it. He mentioned the phrase when he woke her up after the first night they made love. Now, here she was, calmly sitting still while the tattoo artist applied the stencil transfer of Krista's design below the nape of her neck.

It was low enough that no one could see it when she wore her usual clothing. But he would. He liked to see her body—preferably naked. Blake loved that he had that privilege exclusively.

He pulled up a chair and positioned it in front of his girlfriend so he could support her through this sometimes-painful process.

Krista raised her head to receive his kiss and said, "Thanks for coming, hon. Sorry I didn't wait for you. Ronnie here has another appointment after me." She looked over her shoulder to signal to the tattooist to begin.

Despite their uneasy truce about the state of their relationship and his initial objection to her plan to permanently mark her perfectly smooth skin with black ink, Blake lent his strength to Krista. He held her hands, dried her tears, and calmed her down when the screech of the machine got noticeably loud and startled her.

He felt a surge of tenderness when she started to tear up in pain, as the tattooist's needle touched a particularly sensitive area where the bone was close to the skin. The female tattoo artist had a light and steady hand, but he knew the first time under the needle could be rough.

Blake remembered when he and his brothers got the Ryan family crest tattoo—three white griffins on a red background, with the Gaelic clan motto *"Malo mori dam foedari."* Death before dishonor. It was at the same studio where their father obtained his. They all had it drawn in nearly the same location, right in the middle of their broad backs. So the mark could heal, they had it done a month before Aidan was to attend Officer Training School.

Because Aidan had to follow the official Air Force policy regarding body arts, his tattoo was the smallest of the three. Craig's was naturally the biggest—even at sixteen, he was already taller than both of his brothers. He'd easily passed for eighteen. Blake smirked at Aidan's disregard of the requirement that they get their Da's written consent for Craig's tattoo. It was his last act of defiance before he had to adhere to the strictly regimented life of an active-duty US military officer.

Blake knew from the time his brother began his nine-week training that Aidan had lived and breathed not only the US Air Force motto of "Aim High ... Fly-Fight-Win," but also their family's war cry, to die rather than be disgraced.

In his seat before Krista, Blake stretched his legs as much as the cramped space would allow. *I'd rather die than be disgraced.* What a lofty standard to live up to. It relieved him that he'd never needed to prove his willingness to fulfill the slogan; he wasn't sure he could go through with giving up his life for his principles. His relationship with Krista could change that.

Last night, they had agreed to maintain some distance between each other at the office, to negate the rumors about being seen kissing here in Boracay. But secrets had ways of coming out. How they dealt with the upcoming adversity would be a test of their love, if Human Resources made an issue of it. He would rather resign than put Krista through a scandal that could damage her career and hurt her future.

Blake looked down when Krista moaned. "It's okay, baby. It'll be all over soon," he whispered soothingly. Ronnie, the artist, had begun shading on the second "E." Krista was close to having herself a complete tattoo.

"I know, hon," she replied. "It's not the needle. It's you. Your hands are gripping mine too tight."

Blake hadn't realized his disturbing thoughts had manifested themselves and created a tension that translated itself to Krista. He tried to let go of her hand, but she held on.

"I'm fine now. How are you doing?" Her voice was muffled—her head rested on her arms, which were one on top of the other, on the back of the chair.

"I'm all right. I just remembered something." He gently removed his hand from hers. "Sweetheart, would you like me to take a couple of pictures for you before Ronnie applies the ointment? You may want to send them to your friends." The tattoo artist was nodding as he said this. The protective ointment would cause a glare.

"Sure. Kindly pass me my phone." When he did, she pressed her index finger on the pad but didn't hand it to him. "Uhm, honey, is it okay if Ronnie takes the photos?" She motioned him closer and whispered, "I'll show it to you later when it's just the two of us."

Surprised but intrigued, Blake nodded and passed the phone to the tattoo artist after Krista handed it to him. He stepped aside, out of respect for his girlfriend's request, while Ronnie photographed the finished ink. She must have added something to the design before he arrived. No use speculating on it now. He'd find out soon enough.

Blake leaned in the doorway and thought of how far Krista and he had come since Saturday morning. There was her initial antipathy of his careless words of greeting. The jaw-dropping transformation and first kiss. *That hot hammock make-out session.* Then she had gifted him with her virginity. Most recently, she had accepted a committed relationship with him in defiance of her mother. All in one week. All because she had embraced her new motto—*carpe diem. Seize the day.* He could only feel exceedingly happy to be the beneficiary of her resolve to live each day to the fullest.

When he left her last night, he had some time to think and to admit to himself that he might have rushed his ultimatum, just as he'd made a quick judgment about her family on the night of her birthday. His pride took a beating, and he lashed out. All his understanding of her romantic inexperience went out the window the moment an adverse situation appeared. Blake shook his head in regret.

He couldn't wait to make love to her again. He missed doing that last night because of his brooding. He shook his head. *That's all over.* Tonight, he would make up for keeping his distance. He'd take care to be gentle though, for she would still be sore in some areas. But he wanted to make the most out of their last night in Boracay.

He straightened when she approached, her business done with the studio. She carried a bag containing extra oils and ointments that would hasten the healing process. He looked forward to rubbing them on her soft skin later tonight—and every night for the rest of their lives, if she would let him. "Do you want ice cream again, baby?" he offered, exactly like he did last time they were here.

"Always," she beamed up at him. "This time, I want *ube* ice cream on top of *halo-halo* with *leche flan* and *halaya*." There were no tears in her eyes anymore. Only the glint of pride that she had suffered through pain to stamp an indelible reminder of her determination to live on her own terms.

Chapter Twenty-Four

Pag-ibig [pag-ee-big] n. – love.

It's time. Krista told her image in the bathroom mirror.

It was late afternoon by the time they left the tattoo shop, so they decided to come back to Perlas and have their dinner here. Blake even joined her for *halo-halo* ice cream, breaking his no-dessert-at-dinner rule. He had joked and laughed and told her about his own experience, when he'd had the ink tattooed on his back.

To her delight, he'd arranged for the fireworks to be lit tonight instead of Sunday night. On the surface, everything seemed to have returned to the way they were before last night's fight. But they hadn't really talked. *Now, we will.*

Earlier, she'd stopped him from seeing her bold statement. She wanted the reveal to be special. So here she was, wearing the pearls he gave her and nothing else, to make sure no barriers existed between Blake and his view of her declaration.

He'd asked her to model the pearls for him just before Maddie's gift-giving, and after that, her parents caught her in the act of almost kissing Blake.

Ugh. This isn't the time to think about the tear-filled drama from Wednesday night. It's time to finally tell my man I love him.

Krista artfully posed at the door of the bathroom, her hands lifting her hair off her neck to display her jewelry to their most dazzling effect. "Honey, can you please put ointment on my tattoo and change the bandage?" She also knew the stance showed off her curves and long legs to perfection.

***

Blake whistled. "Come here, baby. I've been looking forward to this the whole afternoon long." He went instantly hard inside his boxer briefs.

Krista climbed onto the bed and handed him the After Inked ointment. She sat cross-legged in front of Blake with her back to him and gathered the heavy mass of her hair up on top of her head. Blake gently peeled off the bandage the tattoo artist had applied, and scratched lightly at the adhesive that remained stuck to her skin.

"*Ooooh*. That feels so good," Krista moaned.

A couple of minutes passed quietly while he rubbed the healing oil on her skin. Blake had nearly swallowed his tongue when he saw Krista at her sexiest best. A golden goddess with a sultry smile on her lips and her skin glowing, setting the cranberry pearls off spectacularly; she was the embodiment of his fantasies all those months ago. Krista was centerfold material for sure, but he wouldn't want any other man ogling her. She was for his eyes only.

Krista twisted her hair into a bun and asked, "Honey, do you know what my initials are?"

"Hmm? 'KL'?" Blake answered absently, his mind on what he planned to do to her once she was bandaged again.

"And yours are …?" Krista prodded.

My initials? What? Blake's fingers went still on her back. As if blinders were removed from his eyes, he finally saw what she had been hinting at. *It's right there in front of my face!*

Underneath the words "*Carpe Diem,*" and within the curling vines, were the letters "K" and "L," a heart, and his initials, "B" and "R." He traced the letters and the symbol that expressed her avowal of love for him. "Krista Lopez loves Blake Ryan," he whispered, his voice hoarse with suppressed emotion.

Krista turned and took his face in her hands. She looked in his eyes, and said, "I, Krista Lopez, love you, Blake Ryan. I'm sorry it took me so long to say it. I couldn't say the words before, because I was guilty, scared, and insecure." She placed a finger on his lips to allow her to continue.

"I was feeling guilty because not only was I disobeying my mother, I also initially planned to use you for one week only. Then, I didn't trust that your profession of love for me was real. That it wasn't just the enchantment of Boracay. That what you were feeling would disappear next week when we returned to the real world." She smiled when he shook his head, denying her negative assumptions. Krista gave him a light kiss on the mouth.

She leaned away before he could deepen the kiss. "At the same time, I feared the newness of my feelings for you. Falling in love is one of my most cherished dreams, but I got scared when it happened so fast with you. What if there's a catch? For over a decade I was happy enough to only have my family and friends. A few days with you, and you've suddenly become the center of my life. How do I know it could last beyond this week, this month, and this year?"

Blake had to speak out. "We can't know. We can only work on it together every moment of every day." He dragged her onto his lap. He couldn't stand even the smallest distance between their bodies.

"Exactly," Krista agreed. "Do you know what the full quote of *carpe diem* means?"

"I only know it means to seize the present because you cannot trust that tomorrow will come," he replied, rubbing her back gently.

Krista nodded. "I thought so, too, at first. But I read up on it some more, and it actually means one should not leave the future to chance, but do all they can today to make their future better." She wrapped her arms tighter around him. "You are the only one that will make my future better, Blake. I love you. I want to be yours, and I want you to become mine. Today. For as many todays as we can seize. And I want everyone to know."

Blake felt his throat tighten with emotion. She unmanned him with her words, but at the same time she empowered him with her love. "I love you too, Krista. *Iniibig kita.* More and more each day we're together. I am yours. I have been from the moment you honored me with your first kiss. That you're mine makes me the happiest man in the world right now. I can't wait to let the world know about us."

Tears of joy filled Krista's eyes. She touched his face and whispered, "Make love with me, Blake.

This time, I want nothing to come between us. I want you. All of you." Implicit in her invitation was a promise that she was ready to commit fully to him, ready to create a future with him today.

Blake's heart swelled with happiness. "There is nothing I crave more than to make love with you, Krista." As he told his brother, Krista was The One for him. The woman he would introduce to his family as his future wife and mother of his children. Any child they created would be wanted. *Cherished.*

Their lips met in a sweet kiss that quickly blazed into a full-fledged fire neither tried to douse. Hands roamed, tongues mated, and bodies touched in a timeless dance of lovers who have found in each other the partner of their heart, moving together in a rhythm that matched the beat of love. They were seizing the moment. Making the future better. Today.

SATURDAY

Epilogue

Pamilya [pa-meal-ya] n. – family.

He's nervous. Blake had a tight grip on the steering wheel of his BMW. His knuckles were white, even though the car had been parked in front of her parents' *Bahay na Bato*—a brick and stone Spanish colonial house—for a good five minutes already.

Last night when she told him about her mother's invitation for them to visit today, he'd seemed happy, even excited. They took the first flight out of Boracay and drove for three hours to get here by lunchtime. Knowing her mother, Krista guessed she'd have spent all morning cooking up a storm for her daughter's arrival. It would be a belated birthday celebration.

"Blake." She stroked his arm. "My parents already love you for bringing me home."

He turned to her and smiled. "I hope so." Leaning over, he whispered, "They're watching from the window, right?"

Krista giggled. "My siblings are. My mom's probably as anxious as you, and is very likely pacing in the living room."

"Who's anxious? I'm not anxious," he declared. "I'm tense, edgy, jumpy, nervous as hell.

You are anxious. Me, not so much." The honest admission made them both laugh.

Her boyfriend reached for her hand and kissed it. "Thanks, love. Let's go meet your parents."

Gesturing for her to stay in her seat, he got out and ran to open the door on her side. The gentlemanly conduct would surely earn him points with her dad. After taking the gifts from the back seat, he locked the car. Hand in hand, they walked to the front door, which opened almost as soon as they reached it.

"Happy birthday, *Ate!*" Her brother and sister jostled each other to fight over who got to her first. Farrah won after giving her brother a particularly strong stomp on his foot.

"*Ang gwapo nya, Ate.* Does he have a brother? And, is he as handsome as your boyfriend?" Farrah stage-whispered as they hugged.

Before Krista had a chance to answer, Alex elbowed his sister out of the way to give Krista a bear hug. Her little brother was not so little anymore. He had bulked up and stood as tall as her. She gave him a pat on the back and eased out of his arms when she saw her parents approach. Alex let go of her and approached Blake to shake his hand. Her sister had done the same.

She bent over her father's proffered hand and pressed her forehead to it in the Filipino way of *Mano.* Krista turned to her mother to show the same sign of respect but was surprised when her mother opened her arms wide instead. Tears came into her eyes, and she fell into her mother's embrace. "*Nanay.*"

"Happy birthday, *Anak.*" Her mother stroked her hair. "Don't cry, or I'll start crying, too. We'll never get to eat." She stepped back and looked pointedly at Blake.

Krista held out her hand to Blake, inviting him to step inside the family circle. "*Tay, Nay,* this is my boyfriend, Blake. Blake, my mom and dad."

Blake stepped forward and said, "*Maganda'ng tanghali po, ma'am, sir.*"

Her mother's gasp and her father's nod of approval made her smile. Same with the thumbs-up sign her brother and sister flashed behind their parents. Her boyfriend's Tagalog was once again winning hearts.

Her dad held out his hand for Blake to shake. "Let's not be formal, *Iho.* Call me *Tito* Arsen and Krista's mom *Tita* Marissa." *For now,* was unspoken. With hope, her future husband would be invited to call her parents *Tatay* and *Nanay.*

"*Salamat po, Tito* Arsen, *Tita* Marissa," Blake dutifully replied, bowing his head to each of her parents as he addressed them. He had visibly relaxed since their arrival. The smile on his face was easy, and his arms were loose at his sides.

"*Gutom na ako. Tara, kain na tayo,*" Alex hollered from the dining room. Krista's mother scolded her brother for yelling. Her father just shook his head at his son's antics.

She stroked Blake's back as they walked, and asked, "You okay?"

"I'm great, baby." He smiled down at her. "They're nice—your parents. I like them."

"I told you—" The sight of their dining table, groaning under the weight of the platters and platters of her favorite dishes, brought her up short. *Pancit Malabon, lechon kawali, embutido, menudo, kare kare, lumpiang Shanghai, relyenong bangus, sapin-sapin, maruya,* and rice crowded the long table. They must have closed the *café* early yesterday to prepare all of these. Her parents had owned and ran a roadside eatery since her dad retired from teaching and they moved to her mom's province several years ago.

Krista glanced at Blake. His eyes were big— he seemed impressed with the spread before them. He looked at Krista, eyes twinkling with mirth. She knew she had the same expression on her face. They both had to suppress their laughter. This looked almost exactly like the breakfast he ordered on Tuesday, for her birthday treat. Already he had found something in common with her mother.

When they were all seated, her father led the prayers. Krista hid another smile when they all gaped at Blake as he made the sign of the cross. *My man is hitting three-point shots from all over the floor today.* Beside her, Farrah and Alex were giving her thumbs-up signs again. Krista's heart swelled with happiness. *We're going to be all right. We're going to make it.*

She reached under the table for Blake's hand and squeezed it. He pressed right back but kept his gaze on her parents. "*Tito, Tita,* may I ask for your blessing? I would like to invite Krista to meet my family in the US. I regret that I will be taking her away from you during Christmastime, but it would truly make me happy to spend my birthday with her

231

and introduce her to my loved ones, as she has introduced me to hers." Her parents communicated in that quiet way of theirs. A look passed between them before turning to Blake and nodding. They gave their permission.

He turned to her and said, "This week has been the best of my life so far. Falling in love with you, and knowing you feel the same has been a wish fulfilled. You have honored me by sharing your family with me; please allow me to share mine with you."

Krista brought their joined hands to her lips and looked into his eyes, her own filling with tears. "Yes. Yes, I'll go with you." *Anywhere. Anytime.*

He bent his head towards her and whispered, "They're going to love you as much as I do."

Krista nodded. "I hope so, Blake. I pray so."

###

AUTHOR'S NOTE

Blake's resort Perlas in Boracay is a combination of hotels I've stayed in all over the world. It does not exist in real life. Which means the airstrip in the island itself is also imaginary. As of this book's publication, the closest airport is still in the nearby town of Caticlan, a short boat ride away. That's about the only thing I made up. (And, maybe the horses, too. I'm not sure.) Everything else is true: the fine white sand, the clear waters, blue sky, spectacular sunsets, and the warm hospitality of the people are one-hundred percent real. Go and visit Boracay. Tell them about my book.

I hope you enjoyed Krista and Blake's story. The next book NEW YORK ENGAGEMENT is a sequel. It's a novella set in New York City where they will spend Blake's birthday and the holidays. It's available from your favorite etailers starting May 21, 2018. books2read.com/NewYorkEngagement

You also met Krista's best friend Maddie and Blake's older brother Aidan. Their story is called SINGAPORE FLING. The two of them will help plan Krista and Blake's wedding since Maddie will be Krista's maid of honor and Aidan will stand for Blake as his best man. It's out in stores on October 21, 2019. books2read.com/SingaporeFling

For bonus content, check out my website www.maidamalby.com. You'll find photos of all the places and food I mentioned in the series, as well as sneak peeks of my work-in-progress.

If you have any questions or comments, you can contact me at maidamalby@gmail.com. You can also find me on Facebook (Maida Malby), Twitter (@MaidaMalby) and Instagram (Carpe Diem Chronicles). And if you liked my book, please leave a review. I'd really appreciate it and it'll help new readers find it. Thank you.

Made in the USA
Coppell, TX
28 December 2019